Acknowledgements

Mascara was first published on Laura Hird's website. *Charly* and *Authenticity* were published on the Shortbread website. *The Park* was published in the magazine Pushing out the Boat. *Just Another Day* won the 2010 William Soutar Prize and was published in Northwords Now. *Killing the Monkey* was published in New Writing Dundee.

A previous collection "*Mother Icarus*" was shortlisted by Salt Publishing for their international short story competition The Scott Prize in 2012.

Contents

Of Dogs and Diabetes 7

Mascara 14

Charly 21

Our Own Grande Dame De Paris 27

A Life in Carpets 36

Man Seeks Reasonable Woman 49

Ashes 56

Mother Icarus 69

The Flute 76

Fearlas Mor 83

Lads 92

Pink Wellies 98

Caramel Wafers 105

Here's to Succulence 113

The Park 120

Just Another Day 123

Killing the Monkey 129

Grace's Favour 132

Soft Soap and Dishes Best Served Cold 138

Bashed Noses and Broken Dreams 145

The Camel Coat 151

Jakub's Angel 160

Authenticity 169

Daffodils 176

OF DOGS AND DIABETES

Sometimes she'd bang on the window for ages she said but ah refused to take the door off the snib then. Ah mean, in this street, anybody could've walked in. Ah'm a bit corned beef, among other things, and the trains over the back make a hell of a racket. To be honest, since the wife died, a year ago next month, it just seemed ma life was as shrivelled as a Co-op neep. All ah wanted was peace and quiet. Ah read the paper and that, but after a while, the old eyes would get droopy and ah'd nod off. Thing is, you can nod off for a few seconds and it's as if you've been out for hours. You wake up and wonder where the hell you are. Worse thing is though, you're holding a cup of tea and reading, and before you know it there's a thump, the book's on the floor and the tea's in your crotch. The thing is, you open your eyes and there's this cup tilted at forty-five degrees, as if you've done it deliberately. It was a frame of mind, ah suppose: ah felt like one of those damn trains charging by to Glasgow Central, only mine was heading nowhere. Like that time Mary and me were staying in Sitges and we got a train back from Barcelona. Mary asked a woman if this train was for Sitges and she nodded. So we settled down and off we went. In no time the woman comes swaying her way along the coach frantically waving her arms - 'No! No! El tren para Valencia!' Every mile we went past Sitges seemed like we were heading over the edge of the known world: just being carried where we didn't want to go. Well, it stopped before Valencia and we got off. Mary thought it was funny. Well thank God, ah got off my train too.

Ah'd had a string of so-called Care Assistants and ah was fed up with it. Before she came, every blooming day a new one would appear and start yapping away. 'These crystal bowls are lovely!' Aye, well keep your hands off them and get some dusting done, ah'd be thinking. Half the time they'd just flick their way round an ornament – never lift them. That donkey we bought in Fuengirola had four dust marks where the feet were, Emily told me. Emily. Emily was the first regular.

She usually came about eleven to make me a bite and ah'd let her in. When ah heard the door, that is. She was older than the others, though she wore the same blue overall with the council logo, like a pair of crossed legs. Quite appropriate you might say. McNulty was her name. Emily. Not bad for her age, ah suppose.

'Just be calling me Emily, Mr Moodie,' she said, 'all my clients do.' Clients, ah thought - ah'm a client now! Very racy. With a name like Emily, you imagine a wee lassie with a flowery dress on, not someone who's a size whatever with arms like Raphael Nadal. My Mary was a twelve, ah remember. McNulty never tried to wash me, though. It's my feet ah've got problems with, not lifting a facecloth.

Ah still remember the day the wee Chinese girl from Aberdeen appeared and started running the bath. 'Fit like?' she says, then before ah open my mouth, all ah hear is

'Water's nice and hot Mr Moodie; next time, don't bother to dress before I come.' So ah gets up really slowly, like ah'm John Wayne in a saloon when somebody's mentioned milk, and ah looks at her and ah says

'And what exactly do you think you're doing?' Then she turns and says,

'You've got nothing that I haven't seen before.' The cheeky besom! Well, it turns out she'd got the wrong house and it was Sandy Lovell two doors down that gets a bath. Jesus. Typical council! Apology? You've got to be kidding.

Of Dogs and Diabetes

Ah should explain. Ah'm diabetic. Forty years of it has buggered my feet. The point being, a couple of weeks ago ah didn't feel on for any lunch and ah nodded off, watching the indoor bowling on the telly, and when five-bellies-McNulty came through she couldn't rouse me. Must've been a bit of a shock, right enough, because ah'd taken a bad hypo. She'd been briefed by the office, she said, and she tried to give me the last of the milk but the dog had nudged her and she spilt it. Said she couldn't find a biscuit. She never knew about my caramels then. Anyhow, ah got the usual stuff about regular meals and got kept in overnight.

When ah got back, she came by and told me she'd seen a programme on TV about how dogs were trained to know when their masters were ill.

'God's honest truth,' she says, 'If it's a cold you've got, and they're after hearing you sneeze, they'll go and fetch a tissue.' Amazing!

'Wouldn't be blowing your nose too, would they?' I says. Jesus. The woman's stupid. Well, no, she's not stupid, exactly: more irritating. Irritatingly cheerful, ah would have to say. Which to me, then, could be as bad.

'You know,' she said, 'I was after thinking we could train Tess to be keeping you awake, in case, well, you know…' It sounded daft to me, but for some reason ah said ah'd give it a go. Get off at this station, man, ah thought. Change. She's a Dalmatian by the way - Tess that is - not McNulty, not with that accent, though I have to say it's more slipper than brogue. I mean Tess is a good-sized dog. Ah got her when she was a pup from this guy in the pub who'd found her hanging in a blue Tesco bag. Said he couldn't keep her because his wife had only one leg. So I called her Tess, because ah was reading Hardy at the time.

Anyhow, McNulty made me pretend to be dozing and she held up my foot for the dog as if it was a bloody sausage or something.

'Come on, be biting his foot won't you, wake up that lazy aul' man of yours; he's not after sleeping, he's having a hypo.' Ah'm thinking, oh aye, perhaps she could be drawing the aul' dog a diagram. Tess, who by the way, is a very intelligent dog in my opinion - Tess's probably thinking, a hypo? now would that be anything to do with what that vet stuck in me when I cut my paw that time, or, might it allude to the old boy's propensity for playing dead, and if the latter, perhaps a bit of mouth-to-foot resuscitation would be in order. Well, nothing happened. She's my damned dog, so of course she's not going to bite my foot is she? So Maud Gunne has another go and the dog won't move, just tilting her head, she says, only now she's got her blue ball in her mouth as if this is a great game. Ah did my bit, kept my eyes shut so ah couldn't see a bloody thing but she gave a commentary:

'No, she's just looking at me Mr Moodie, she's not going to bite you.' Then she shouts at the dog – 'Your man's dying! He's dying! And you just sitting there!' Well, the dog begins to get excited and starts barking and drops the ball and she's jumping up on McNulty yapping and play-biting her arms and said McNulty panics and she starts jumping too. Jesus. And all the time ah'm just sitting there pretending to be playing dead, when out of the blue McNulty grabs my right leg and shoves it in the dog's mouth and the bugger bites me. A sore one, even for my numb toes. Ah leap up from the chair – not a thing ah was known for, unless the Celts had scored and my coffee cup goes arse-over-tit all over the dog. She calms down, shakes herself and then there's coffee skitters all over the telly and the wall. What a stushie! McNulty just laughs and says,

'Take your trousers off and I'll be rinsing them.'

A couple of days later ah get a visit from Social Work.

'Just a routine visit,' says this woman over her half-moons. 'Would mobility be an issue?' An issue! Everything's a bloody issue these days.

'No,' I say, 'Getting about is not an issue.' Just being bothered's the issue, ah say to myself. McNulty, ah think. Ah'll swing for her yet. Then Mother Theresa spots those persistent coffee stains and she says,

'Are you prone to taking falls, Mr Moodie?' Jesus. "Prone to taking falls!"

'No, ah'm not prone to anything, madam.' ah say, really angry, and she points at the wall and raises where her eyebrows should be.

'Coffee,' ah say. 'Ah spilled coffee. Ah fell over the dog.' Knew ah'd never get rid of her if ah told the truth.

'The dog? Isn't it a bit dangerous to have such a big dog when you're a little unsteady on your feet?' She went soon after, just before ah reached for the hammer, said she'd be in touch.

Well, the next day ah nodded off again and woke up to discover ah'd sprouted a dog-extension to my foot. Tess was tugging at it as if it was a stick. Ah'm still groggy and ah'm pulling my Superman slipper away and the blighter keeps tugging and ah'm trying to pull her off and McNulty walks in from the kitchen. ' Dozing!' she says. Jesus. Ah' m seventy-three. If you canny doze at seventy-three when can you? It's a wee treat. It's God's way of making life bearable. It's that snidey way women say things: it felt as if ah'd been caught looking at a nude picture of Petula Clark or something. No wonder you can't sleep at night, she says, and ah think, that's just a shot in the dark.

'Look, she's got my bloody foot!' ah shout, 'Get her off my foot!' So she grabs Tess's collar and yanks her off. Jesus! So why, you wonder, would Tess want to grab my foot? You got it in one. Now that dog thinks every time ah nod off, ah've to get my life saved. She's a four-legged McNulty now, for God's sake.

Well, from the ashes of pensioner abuse, ah have to admit, a wee phoenix has risen - ah'm getting out more. McNulty the wise, said she thinks ah should take the dog out every time ah feel drowsy, and if it's that or losing a foot - for ah wouldn't feel a thing while it was being ripped to shreds - ah'm game for a stroll. She is getting a bit podgy, ah have to admit.

Ah started going out for walks round the block then the other day it was raining so I took Tess a bit further up the hill and dropped into The Flying Scotsman for a wee hauf. Dead. Not a dicky-bird. They've got this huge screen and every time you look up there's some young lassie in gold hot-pants swinging her bum about and urging you to eat more oven chips. At one time, when I'd drop in with Mary, Old Charlie or Eddie Wilson would be sitting in a corner over a nip and a hauf but Charlie took a stroke at the Dogs and I haven't seen Eddie since that night Celtic were thumped in Bratislava. Ah've a feeling he went home and did himself in. Ah've some sympathy too. Eddie was Celtic daft.

Well ah sat like a stookie and drew McNulty's phizog in the head of ma Guinness and watched the rain on the window while the young guy was sticking his dirty rag into sloshed-out glasses. Enough to put you off your drink, that. Then ah went to wipe my nose and two sweeties fell out my hanky. Chocolate caramels! Ah'm thinking, how did they get there? Ah keep a wee stash in a tin on the telly and take one when ah feel like it. Then ah remember McNulty saying ah should always have something sweet with me and she didn't mean her. Jesus. Ah looked at her and she winked. Well ah ate one of the caramels anyway, though the beer tasted hellish afterwards. Ah suppose it was a kind thought, right enough.

Ah got hassle when ah went through the park on the way back, though. The rain was off so ah thought ah'd give Tess a wee run. She's off like a shot chasing a ball that this man's chucking to his wee girl and the wee lassie panics and starts crying when Tess lollops up. Ah could see father wasn't too pleased and Tess runs off with the bloody ball which made matters worse. 'Can't you control your dog chum?' he says, really sniffy, and all ah can do is say ' Sorry.' Ah got the ball and threw it back to them, and it bounced off the guy's shoulder, and he turns with a look on him, and ah shout, 'Really, really sorry.' like some idiot. Ah'm mad now though and when ah turn round Tess's performing on the grass and there's a family watching her doing it. God, if there's one thing ah hate about having a dog these days it's lifting poop. Ah've no bag of course, only my hankie, so ah think, damn it, ah'll be in trouble if ah don't do this. So ah spread it out and lift this squishy pile. Ah'm nearly boaking with the stink and ah just stroll off with this hanky full of muck. Ah can feel it seeping too.

At the gate ah dump the hanky in a bin. Then ah smell my hand. Jesus. It smells vile, so ah walk down the road, dog on lead now, stinky hand rigid by my side and ah'm thinking ah'll put McNulty in her place with a wee handshake, when who comes up the street but the lady herself. Her head's down and she's walking fast swinging that basket thing she carries.

My arm's up and ah'm just about to proffer a long-delayed hand of friendship when ah see her face. Got this scared look in her eyes.

'I'm sorry John,' she says, peching, 'It's my son. The Office phoned. He's had an accident. I'm after having to leave early. There's a wee casserole in the oven though, so you'll not be starving.' Jesus. Ah heard an echo - John! She called me John! Ah hold my hand up and say 'It stinks of poo.'

'How's that?' she says, and ah tell her and she digs in her bag and scooshes some perfume on my palm and rubs it in. She said something but ah couldn't hear it for a train. As she was doing it though, ah smelt her hair, and ah thought of Mary.

'Ah'll leave the door off the snib!' ah shouted after her, and all ah could smell was roses.

MASCARA

He should have been back yesterday. 'Phone me,' Muriel always said as he left, but this time, she was getting Shona ready for school and he had to get off. There had been hot words the night before and a night staring at her broad back, so he just left it.

On the way North to Aberdeen, he chewed wine gums and had one of those Damascene moments when the whole thing becomes clear: not a holy vision kind of thing but a realisation that this was it. This was him, the measure of the man, one Ron Reid, purveyor of hardware sundries, a man in a cheap suit and black scuffed shoes with a car full of plastic tat that defied decomposition. Oh, but he was good at this. North Division Salesman of the Month God knows how often. And let's face it the stuff is good tat; durable, attractive, and so on. Sells itself.

Well, the deal was done, though the order like most those days was cut. Times were hard, takings down. The way it was then. He couldn't face the car, so he went for a pint or two.

Nice wee pub by the river. Dark little tables with those cast iron legs that would outlive Armageddon and a sloppy top with rings intersecting like some kind of Olympic orgy. Stuffing oozing from the leather banquette. Sun through the window warm on his face. A packet of salt and vinegar crisps. He was happy. Watched the come and go of regulars; the glances, the craic between the two barmaids who knew the old boys with their collies or the bald young ones hefting their snooker cues. Before he knew it, the day was fading and the thought came that he'd drunk too much to drive back. That and the notion that he'd steal a day that didn't belong to him in the world of the father and husband. He pulled out his mobile, and mid dialling thought, No. I'm my own man. I don't need this fucking umbilical cord of responsibility. Trust me. Just trust me to be OK.

He got himself a B & B with plastic daffies on the sill and clean curtains up. The woman seemed pleasant and said she'd a room on the first floor overlooking the Railway line. Blue candlewick, a picture of canoes in the sunset; the usual, but cheap. He told her he'd bring his stuff later and took the key on a weight that could kill.

Now the road rolls under him, pulling him where he doesn't want to go. He'd phoned in the morning telling her he'd broken down and had to stay over. She was OK. Now he has to pull over, can't face her yet, not the way things are. Can't let her look into his eyes. Not yet. Got to gather himself, rehearse the lines of the Theatrica Domestica, before he goes on stage. It's the little things that will get him: the 'Why didn't you?' and the 'Surely you could have' while he practises the big answers. He can see her at the door; those jeans, those tops she wears that all look the same. If you didn't know better, you wouldn't look twice, but she's his, and he knows better. Hasn't been plain-sailing, but when the storms pass he knows they're stronger, more resilient and it takes a fiercer storm to shake them next time. The car's full of the other one, the stranger, her presence pervasive as the stink of vomit.

He sniffs her perfume on his sleeve, her smell on his flesh. The car's full of it: on the seats, on the handle there, on the clip of the glove compartment. Thank Christ she didn't smoke. He showered that morning like his life depended on it but it's still there. Water isn't enough. The traffic drives him on: tailgating lunatics with their cases full of whatever shit they peddle, in and out and in and out.

He turns hard left. It's a quarter-past twelve and the sun's edging each cloud like a drunk's morning eyes. He pulls into a parking spot with a sign. Needs more time to think, to feel his way free. There's a choice of walks: two, three or six miles. He takes the three. Fuck this. Here he is in the middle of nowhere on a sunny evening when he should be sitting out the back having a Becks and watching the kids on the trampoline. He walks, feeling the muscles in each thigh complaining. Not fit. Too much sitting behind that damn wheel. A woman passes with a white Cairn and smiles. Why do all middle-aged women feel they have to smile at you? You don't have to smile missus, I'm not going to rape you. Just pass by, go to your cosy wee house, watch the dog lap from its bowl and call to the old man that you're home. He'll be so bloody grateful that you haven't been raped again tonight. God, his head's away somewhere. He's so fucking angry. Why did he do it? Why didn't he just stop, just stop for a micro-second and think about this - the afters. But no. Another couple, another dog. A Weimaraner loping along like a wolf, sniffing every tree but keeping to the path. That's a good lesson - sniff all you like but keep to the path: the path of matrimony, the path that promises lay, the path that means you don't have to feel like this. They're arm in arm on the path just away with each other. Young. Lucky bastards. Just you and me darling, on this lovely evening in these lovely woods and back home to the lovely telly. Yes, that's what he'd like right now - boring loveliness.

He's getting this feeling of being where he shouldn't; can imagine some hi-tech camera in the sky transmitting to a computer. Not so much Google Earth as Google Man. Just key in "Daddy" or "Husband" and then watch as it scans the globe whirling round and round and you drag that wee mouse closer and closer towards the earth and then you see Scotland and then you move to the centre and then you're in Perthshire and bingo you're coming in to land on a lone figure walking along this track and…

'Look, it's Daddy!

'No, it can't be. Daddy's on his way home from Inverness. His car broke down and it'll be fixed now. He'll be here soon.'

'It is. It is. It's his jacket. Look …'

'God, so it is.'

'Let's talk to him.'

'No. We can't do that…'

Thank Christ it's fantasy. Ten years down the road who knows. Then we'll all be so scared of putting a foot wrong we'll all be perfect little people. He'd settle for that right now. To be so shit scared of being caught that there's nothing left to be caught for. A bloody great moral dome that covers every moment of our lives like The Eden Project - The Sturgeon Project - a moral umbrella, free to the people of Scotland.

He leans against a tree. Last time he did this he'd been dumped by a fat girl he thought he couldn't live without. Now he sees another woman, the pock marks on her face still visible under her slap. She's there at the bar leaning, solid and calm in the midst of the hubbub, the talk and laughter, the gush of draught, the clinking, the pop of corks. And him, bored and alone, his room key bulging his pocket. 'Is that your room key or are you just glad to see me?' He laughs to himself. Always alone. It's his job to travel alone, to offer words, get the orders and then be alone again in some grotty B & B with nylon sheets and stains on the wall by your head. Each room is its own story but it leaves wee signs here and there: the spots on the ceiling where a can exploded in a gush; the fag dropped from the washbasin on to the carpet and left for a second to bite its brown hollow; the fag stains like shit on the bottom of the shower. I mean what sort of cretin showers with a fag in his mouth? With him it's the light more than anything. The light at night may come through the thin curtains from a streetlamp or a neon sign or there may be no light, just a city darkness that's without stars or hope and in the morning you wake dimly to objects that are in the wrong place: a wall that shouldn't be there, your brain tells you, till it clicks into gear for another day and you know where you are.

If the bar hadn't cleared. If she hadn't been left standing there with her back to him showing those legs. It was the way her calves swelled. Bare calves. He wanted to touch them. In his head he did. He was stroking them and that told him how smooth they were. If he could have touched them for the price of a drink, he wouldn't have needed more. She was leaning on her elbows and her arse was sticking out. A woman's arse! He went for another drink and she turned and smiled at him. She broke into him like a burglar breaks into a house. She cut her way soundlessly into his loneliness with the silence and the skill of a smile. Christ, why did she have to do that. And he was burgled. It's Muriel though: she's the one that's been burgled. He's what he's always been, but now he's not what she thinks he is; what she thinks the core of him is. He's not the guy she nags and fights and hug and cooks for; buys oven chips for because she knows he likes them, when she hates them: He's not the guy she strokes when those tender moments come - when a glimpse of his neck or his wrist or his knee turns her insides to mush with love and he wonders what's caused it. He's not the guy she'll be happy with when his hair goes, his hands spot, his ears and nose fur up, his eyes lose their light in a watery film and his dick can't rise to it. What he was, he is no longer.

When he spoke, the old way of talking to a woman kicked in. It was so easy. She listened to his bullshit tales about travelling all the while staring at him with those made-up eyes. Funny thing was, her mouth didn't seem to be interested. It was as if it was telling the real story. Get me another drink it seemed to be saying. He told her she'd smudged her mascara and she touched the wrong eye at first and he said 'No, the other side,' and she laughed as she dabbed the right one. That was the moment when something broke in him. Before that, he knew what was

Mascara

happening. He was looking down on himself. It was a bit of fun, chatting up some strange woman in a strange town. He'd done it before of course; you do when you're on the road. You're tired and with a few in you, you become chatty. Doesn't take long if they're remotely interested. Something about bars: the noise, the hubbub that steals words and leaves looks. And you get close to be heard. The warm breath; the aromas of gin or whisky, the scent. Sometimes he thought of an invitation, but something always happened, like the sudden appearance of a friend, a husband, God even once a phone call that her daughter had been taken to hospital. But this time, the laugh did it. Even her accent was strange: not the inflections he was used to. She wasn't educated or smart, just nice and listening and it was fine. Until the mascara. He thinks if he hadn't mentioned it, everything would have cooled down and they'd have gone their separate ways. He had his room and it was pissing down outside. He'd just come in for the sound of voices and a couple of pints. But he crossed a line and couldn't go back. It was like selling: you cross a line and then you know you'll get the order. Well, he got the order for a back seat job at the edge of the sea. Turned out she was married but the bastard was hitting her. That's what she said. She was lonely she said. Just like that. As she was about to tip a gin down her throat, she stopped, looked at him and said 'I'm lonely.'

Well, he's seen enough films to know the language. No subtitles required, thank you very much. This guy isn't stupid. They drove. Him with two or three pints too. Madness. She gave him directions through town, out along by the river and along the boulevard, the supply ship's lights like fallen stars. They moved into the back. He remembered thinking back to Muriel, even then as he came: the time they were caught by a policeman.

She was very quiet all through as if what she'd hoped for hadn't happened. Oh not the sex, it was more than that - it was as if this made the loneliness worse, this sitting slumped with a stranger with nothing to say that was tender. As if the touching, the stroking, the thrusting had sharpened the senses and the last great sense, if it is one, if emotion is a sense, had disappeared. Emotion left the cinema at half-time. He remembered the Latin saying that after sex, animals are sad. He felt it now. Not with Muriel: with her they'd joke about the wet patch and he'd cuddle her and she'd tease him about the twenty minutes not needing to be timed. Now words were running out.

She wanted to get home she said, so they drove back into town and he dropped her near the pub. She opened her handbag and shook her head. 'Shit, that bastard's cleaned me out. You couldn't let me have a couple of quid could you?' He didn't argue. The memory of their coupling still hot and hellish, he'd lost the confidence to debate issues, to question motives. He gave her twenty and closed the door behind her. She tottered off pulling at her skirt and disappeared through a door. He knew then that it had been a game.

And now, game or no game, he's still at this tree as if it's the only solid thing in the world. His car, his skin, ready to spill the beans. His brain rumbles on like thunder far off that goes and then comes again. He knows. He knows, and that's what matters. If Muriel never knows, what's the difference? All he can do now is go back: take what's left of himself back and brush a tiny smudge of mascara from his soul.

CHARLY

I told mother dear I really, really didn't want to go but she said it would be fine when we got there. I was having a scratchy day and my arms were going red. Oh great. It was only two days after the squirrel episode so I thought I'd better try to be good and not make a fuss. Up in my room, I put on black knee-highs and a red dress that looked odd enough to be OK. Just the sort of thing Janet might wear – not. So that's fine. You could see the scar on my left knee quite clearly. I liked that. My war-wound. 'I see you've made a special effort darling,' said mother. Never lets you down, my mother.

Janet was my friend once, but when I shook the ladder that day and she fell and broke her arm it kind of spoiled things a bit. No-one blamed me apart from Janet because there was no-one else there and when she told everyone that I'd shaken it, I denied it of course. Mum believed me too but there was a funny look on her face as if something was wearing thin. I don't know why I shook it really, I just remember looking up at her blue knickers and that smug little face looking down and I wanted to frighten her. She wasn't really into ladders and things and you'd think she'd climbed Everest or something with that look on her face. Frightened me a bit when I saw her arm though. Didn't know arms could bend like that. Like a bendy toy I once had.

She wouldn't speak to me after that and it's only because our mums are friends that I was invited. Can't imagine Janet was too pleased that I was coming to her Biffday Bash. Would you believe that's what the invitation said: "Biffday Bash?" I could just see us all traipsing up the drive, her mum and her at the door just waiting to get their hands on the presents, all the put-on smiles from everyone. Janet is rich, by the way. She lives in one half of this house surrounded by ginormous trees and a drive full of big chunky cars that her dad drives. It used to be the one house and my dad told me it had belonged to this really cool family that everybody hated called the Varleys or something. He said strange things happened there during the Second World War. Janet's step-dad, Peter, is a doctor. He's OK really, even if he does fancy mum a bit, which is a bit icky really. The odd thing was, Janet actually smiled at me and said she was really glad I'd come and it seemed almost true. Weird. Like, why?

In the lounge, it was mayhem. A cat's chorus of pink girly voices screeching and fluttery little hands tearing away at pink starry wrapping paper. Everywhere was pink. I hate pink. Black for me. Then when all the parcels had been opened and the trash gushed over, our birthday girl, with a horrible blue bead thing round her neck that somebody had given her, rounded us up like sheep to take us upstairs. I caught mum's eye and she scowled. My God, I don't want to be here but I'm supposed to put on this gross act and just get on with it, otherwise…

Upstairs, past the horrible oil paintings which her granddad did, we all disappeared into her bedroom which is the size of our classroom practically. My room is quite small really, just enough space for a bed, a chest of drawers and my table which I think is fine but you'd get four of my rooms in here. You wouldn't believe the stuff she's got. My God, she's got at least three laptops and a huge telly and iPads and phones not to mention posters of some geek called Justin Bieber everywhere, which figures.

She asked if anyone wanted to play something on the Wii but nobody said anything so she opened the window and shouted down to her dad. Couldn't hear what she said, I was too busy examining her iPad, which I couldn't get to work. Monica Wales whispered to me to leave it alone, I'd only drop it, so I put it down and gave her a look. Everybody seems to think I'm good at "looks." That little bitch is one of the sneakiest beings on this planet, and I knew she'd start squealing if I didn't put it down. I didn't know many of them, only Monica and another couple of girls who used to play with me at break. Sarah, Janet's best friend is OK really, but she's always trying to get in with the in-crowd as if she doesn't really have a mind of her own. Well, she doesn't.

Anyway, there I was, trailing after ten frilly creatures charging down the stairs to the garden where her old man has been tending the barbecue. All you could smell was smoke and burning. There were chairs everywhere and wobbly tables with bread-sticks and sausages and dips and bowls of crisps and things stuck on sticks like olives and gherkins, which I do in fact like, though mum says my breath smells like a damp foot if I eat too many. And of course heaps of bottles of horrible fizzy stuff.

So we all found a table and sat and ate and Janet actually sat beside me and said she liked my dress. Sarah nodding like some idiot in agreement. God! I mean when a joke becomes serious you're a bit lost. Then Janet's dad called us out when a burnt burger was ready to be put in a buttered roll. After the first sausage hit Monica, I knew what was coming so I slipped away to wander round the garden which goes in a big "S" shape. I was out of sight of them all and just poking about when I saw the swing. It was just a stick tied to a rope hanging from this big branch so I tucked my dress between my legs and backed up the bank to get a good swing. I was having a great time just singing to myself and hoping no-one would come when I heard this voice in the rhododendrons.

'Charly! Charly, come here.' I knew it was Janet's voice but there was someone else there too. I got off the swing and went into the bush. Janet and Sarah were standing there with this smug look on their faces.

'We've got a secret. Do you want to know what it is?'

Now I'm not really into "secrets," like a box under some cobwebby stairs with a treasure map in it or my little cousin Billy whose secrets were always smelly dead things, but something about the way they looked at each other made me curious. Besides, it was better than eating burnt burgers or wandering around the garden on my own, so I said I didn't mind. The rhodies were kind of thick on the outside but when you went into them, there was quite a bit of room to move about. They bent down a bit and moved deeper in, and I followed, my hand just in front of my eyes to avoid blinding myself. We came out of the bush and then crossed a patch of grass and up some ancient steps. I thought that they'd made a den or something where they escaped to with a bottle of juice and a packet of crisps, but when they stopped there was a concrete platform with a rusty lid thing in the middle.

'Is this your secret then?' I asked, a bit disappointed, really. 'What is it?'

'It's our secret house' said Jane. 'Well, my secret house anyway. I think you'll like it. What do you think, Sarah, should we let her into our house?' I couldn't believe this. It was like something from some of these shows for kids on TV. But I put my hands together pleading with them. I'd just play their game.

'I'm not sure. Has she been good enough?' Jesus. What a pantomime. I decided I'd bluff them.

'Oh well, if you don't really want me to see it…' And I turned round to walk back.

'All right then, come on,' said Janet. 'Let's open her up.'

Janet stuck a wooden pole through the rusty ring in the middle of the plate and holding an end each, she and Sarah managed to lift the lid up. I knew they'd done this before by the way it worked and the fact that the stick was lying nearby. I was pretty excited at the thought of going down underground to see their hideout so I moved forward and peered in.

'We'll go in first. It's our house,' said Janet and she and Sarah eased down the short metal ladder. You couldn't see much at first but when I got down, I saw that it was a room with a concrete floor. It was big enough to hold two old kitchen chairs and a box which was a table. There were three candles in saucers and a wilted flower in a jar. They'd put an old rug on the floor and there was a tin with biscuits in it.

'Well, what do you think?' said Sarah. 'Pretty good eh?'

'It's great, 'I said, and I really meant it. I'd have loved a hidey-hole like this. 'Who made it?' I asked.

'We don't know, but my dad, my real dad, thinks it's something to do with the war. I didn't want him to know when I found it, but he did know of course. He said he didn't want me playing in it.' Janet's face looked odd in the half-light from the sky above the hole. She kept turning to look at Sarah. It was then it dawned on me: they'd brought me here to trap me. Maybe they planned to shut me in here forever. The more I stared at them, the more scared I became. What an idiot I'd been to let them bring me here. I had to get out but not seem too panicky, as if I knew what they were up to.

'I think Dad thought we'd never open it, but we did. Peter's too busy to come out here and mum's only interested in her charities so no-one bothers us,' said Janet. I began to get a bit twitchy.

'OK. It's great, it really is. Wish I had a den like this.'

'Do you want a go then?' said Janet, glancing at Sarah. 'I mean, to be alone in it? You need to be alone really to sort of get the atmosphere.'

'No, it's OK. I get the picture. I mean it's really fun having a place like this but I think we'd better get back to the party. It's your party Janet - they'll wonder where you are.'

'Yes, maybe we should get back,' she said. 'There's a guy coming to do some tricks and stuff at four o'clock. Come on Sarah, we'll go up first.

But I was already at the ladder and started climbing when I felt a slight tug at my ankle then the relief of fresh air on my face. It had been a bit smelly down there with the damp and wax from the candles. I was safe. Birds and sky. As I turned, I saw Sarah's hair appear. My feet seemed to think for me and I found myself pushing down that head. I saw her eyes flash then she seemed to disappear in slow motion. A muffled scream came from down below like some devil from the depths. 'My God! My God, Sarah. Are you Ok?' Janet. Just the same sound she'd made at the foot of the tree.

I dragged the lid over the hole by sitting on the ground and pulling it, and at last, it dropped with a thud. Back through the bushes and there was the swing. Back and forwards, back and forwards I went and the clouds rushed over my head. I'd let them out after a while. Bitches. Trying to scare me. After a time, my mother came and found me.

'How are your arms?'

'Fine. When I'm busy, I forget.'

'Can't you just try a bit harder to play with the others Charly? Just make some effort. And look at your dress! What have you been doing – it's filthy. '

'Nothing much. Just playing houses. Is the entertainer here yet?'

OUR OWN GRANDE DAME DE PARIS

I am fifty-four – she is seventy-four. I wonder what they must think – the two of us here on the *terrace* watching passersby on the Rue du Cardinal Dubois. Am I some ageing gigolo and she my meal-ticket? Earlier, pouring coffee, the old woman who hovers around Marjorie's apartment like some malevolent spectre had given me a strange look that hinted anger. '*Elle est fou*' was all I got from Marjorie when I mentioned it. Perched there opposite me on the rattan chair she sips her *café crème* and dabs her garish lips with a flash of that insouciance that has attracted me from my early years. Her eyes are behind a veil attached to a ridiculous little mauve hat not much bigger than a fascinator. Rarely out of her hand for long is her gilt-edged mirror which she tilts this way and that, her eyes moving with it. Her public grooming has become an affectation: it's as if every gesture, every tilt of the head is an act for some imagined audience. The face which was once beautiful has melted under a mask of makeup, the hair perfectly coiffured but too stiff, like her, too unyielding when the winds of age are howling. She wears fishnet stockings I notice and her toenails are green. While my mother, a couple of years younger, but still fresh-faced and bright-eyed, pours cups of beige tea for tourists in Pittenweem, the girl who shared her bedroom in that cottage near the sea, has contrived a life of ease and sophistication. I suspect only Mika her little Shih Tzu ever hears the creaks and groans that age exacts. For the world, she strides the streets, head held high, nodding to shopkeepers and prostitutes alike as the *grande dame* of the Rue Foyatier. Did I hear a giggle or two as we descended those infernal steps?

L'Espace is quiet again today: Max hovering like some bored crow; Walter, the German, slowly polishing a teapot. Not much call for the *chocolat chaud* today as it is August and Paris has floated South. What's left here is a notion of Paris only, for the city's soul has fled with its inhabitants. I fold Le Figaro, only occasional words of which mean much, but the handling makes me feel French. Marjorie tells me I fool no-one. I remark on the empty tables. She stares and permits a slow smile. She removes her absurd shades and leans towards me conspiratorially,

'I hope, Eric, the wee lemmings get skin cancer from sitting on the Promenade des Anglais.'

'Well, that's a charming thought. Aren't they wise to escape the heat?'

'What heat? It's not a patch on 1940 when you-know-who arrived with his goose-stepping psychopaths. All the rats left the sinking ship.'

'But you weren't here then.'

'Of course I was, my boy. *La Résistance. C'est moi. Toujours. Toujours.*' I laughed at the ridiculous notion of a two-year-old child in The Resistance.

'Weren't they the wise ones? Must have been hell for those left.'

'Going through hell is good *pour l'âme.*'

With her coterie of English friends, she retains her perfect English, the occasional Scotticism a dab of scent behind the ear for my delectation. She'd been a language teacher in Edinburgh when she married the son of the Consul who also joined the consular service and off she went across the globe to inhabit elegant if fading houses in hot places. Her visits home were grand occasions in the Kingdom of Fife: Auntie Madge (Marjorie proving too long for infants' tongues, its abbreviated form stuck) was coming and Madge always brought gifts of chocolate for the children and odd-looking jewellery for my mother. She was beautiful then, and one of my early erotic memories is of her leaning over me to kiss me goodnight and my hand accidentally touching the silky smoothness of her stocking.

As soon as she'd come, she'd be off again. We never saw Paul, her husband, until years later when I was married myself with two children and they were living in retirement in Paris. We'd spend a few days with them on our way East. I never really liked Paul whom I found rather too polite. There was an arrogance about him that never let you forget how important he thought himself and latterly he became just that, as the French Ambassador in Tehran. In retirement, he'd had a heart attack while playing tennis in the Luxembourg Gardens and a delay in treatment had affected his chances of recovery. I can still remember that white room in the Clinique Pasteur and the sight of her, elegant as ever in a white chiffon dress dabbing his beaded forehead. It was August then, and the heat was oppressive that year. Well, he died a few months later in their apartment but we didn't go to the funeral.

Since then, twenty years have passed. My children Lewis and Marissa have made their own lives and I've messed up mine. Too many trips to buy paintings: too many hotel rooms; too many bars and too many conversations with lonely women. I was divorced and moved to Edinburgh where I made a good living with my gallery until the recession hit. I'd always pushed young up-and-coming artists at affordable prices but while the rich were still rich, middle incomes had hit hard times and they stopped buying art. I sold up and moved to a cottage in East Lothian where I now live with my partner Celia and Meph, our border collie. During the hard times when my wife Kate turned into a fire-breathing dragon intent on my destruction, Marjorie was the only one to offer me some consolation. She'd write letters full of news about her grand life but also scolding me for being a fool and a knave for hurting Kate. She once wrote that she'd always suspected that fresh-faced little boy with the mischievous grin would have trouble with women. After that, she'd sign off with a flourish of ' *a bientôt, roué'* which in a stupid way rather tickled me.

So here I am. Summoned this time. The sun has broken through and Celia texted this morning to tell me a ferocious wind had downed our neighbour's ancient ash. More light for us and firewood for him - it's a strange world. Odd, how, every time I come here to see Marjorie something noteworthy happens back home. During a visit with Celia, Kate died in a road accident two years ago with her new husband Michael, and the children's hurt at the separation turned to a kind of mute hatred of me as if I were the cause of her death. No communication with either Lewis or Marissa after, though I think Marissa influences him in some way. He is a placid man whose life revolves round his research into M.S. Now I have only Celia and Marjorie. I've been here for four days now and still don't know the reason for my visit. When I broach the question, she says '*Rien ne presse.*' The placating palm explains all.

She gestures to Max and rummages in her bag in a desultory way, her hands open in exasperation. I take out money and she says 'There's my boy,' snatching twenty francs. Max winks at me. She goes inside and emerges five minutes later with a small bag. 'A wee treat for Mika,' she explains. She shoulders the chain of her bag and we set off home again. At a *pharmacie* she buys something "to knock me out, if you must know, cheri," then we take a taxi back to her apartment. I pay again. She pours two large gins and vermouth then disappears, closing the door. Mika plants herself beside me. She emits an odour of wet clothes. Her friendship moistens my hand.

When I arrived, Marjorie was engaged in some business with her accountant so I sloped off to the Louvre on the off chance that the usual tide of humanity might have ebbed a little. Unfortunately, Japan had spilled half of its population into the centre of Paris and it was hell. I crossed to the Left Bank as I always do and got into conversation with a Swedish woman who wanted to buy the same book as myself. She got a well-bound English translation of Zola's *Germinal* and I got to take her for coffee. The deal was a *café noir* together. What can I say but that we got on well…

The door opens and Marjorie returns in tight jeans and a denim top with sequins. She's dressed for a cruise of the Caribbean or perhaps it's Western Night at some church hall in cafe. She scoops up Mika and lowers herself into the deep and ailing armchair opposite. She lights a cheroot and follows a curl of blue smoke towards the scalloped ceiling.

'Eric. I have a wee Scottish favour to ask.'

I shrug, imagining a task easily performed. 'I'm all ears.'

'No. Not so fast. This is not easy. The favour. Not easy for you, I mean.'

'What is it then? You'd like some money?'

'I want you to kill someone.' Slight pause, but only slight – I'm attuned.

'Ah. OK. No problem.' A series of odd remarks had inured me to a newly acquired eccentricity that bordered on the bizarre. I was ready. 'Give me the gun and she's as good as dead.' She smiled, stubbed out the cheroot and moved to the Louis XIV dresser. She opened a drawer and returned with a Luger. Unmistakeably a Luger.

'My God, Marjorie. What the hell…'

'It's a gun, Eric.'

'Yes I can see that. But what are you doing with a gun?'

'It's Paul's. **Was** Paul's. He bought it in Tehran when the trouble started. Not long before Paul died he brought home a business acquaintance that he'd known in his early days in The Service. This man was in love with me. Can't blame him for that, can we darling, but he wouldn't take 'no' for an answer. He started following me. What do they call it now – stalking? Yes, stalking. Every time I'd leave the apartment he'd be there behind me. He wouldn't speak – he'd just walk. And at night, as I pulled the drapes, he'd be out there just looking up. Sometimes he'd wave. Paul knew nothing of this. When they met they'd go for a drink and sometimes they'd come back here. I said nothing. Paul wasn't well then and I didn't want him agitated. I wrote to this man and threatened to tell his wife but it didn't deter him. After Paul died, I thought of leaving here but I decided I wouldn't let him win. I had a friend put dog-shit in the air vents of his car. I even started phoning his wife in an effort to turn the tables. One morning, I found myself answering questions in the *Gendarmerie*. I was the stalker! They let me go with warnings about my conduct. For a long time he stopped his torture but two weeks ago I saw him again out there. Just watching. And today as we sat in the cafe I saw him across the street. I hoped your presence might put him off in some way, but it seems not. Eric, I can't go on like this.' She pushed Mika away, put her slender hands over her face and became immobile for a few seconds. Posing again? When she lowered them, I saw the face I'd last seen at Kate's funeral. It was as if her normal demeanour was some silly mask and this demented, ravaged red-eyed visage was the real one. I moved to her on my knees and clasped her hands. Her mouth was open and her breath was tobacco and gin. I looked at her and told her I couldn't do anything with the gun.

'Marjorie, I feel for you. This must be hell. What you're asking me to do is mad. I'm not a murderer. I can't shoot someone I don't even know. There must be another way.'

'There is,' she said. 'You push me from the balcony. An accident. It's over.'

I got up and poured myself another gin. First shooting, now the balcony. She was serious. The method didn't matter – at the heart of her she meant to do something final.

'Look, let's go for a stroll,' I said, 'The Sacre Cœur, the Tuileries, the Luxembourg - anywhere.'

She sighed then nodded. I replaced the gun, the first I had ever handled. The street was deserted apart from a pissing dog and a couple of small boys. There was no man standing anywhere. She clung to my arm till it hurt.

'Marjorie there's no-one watching you. Look around.'

'Not yet. *Mais plus tard*. He'll come later. Come.' She took my arm and we walked at a steady pace towards Les Halles to see the macaws. Five minutes later it started to rain. Small questioning drops that gradually became statements. We continued walking till she stopped under a tree. I joined her, cursing the fickleness of the weather. She began humming a tune I didn't know, beating time with her head. Her spun hair held droplets like little pearls. It was then that she nudged me.

'It's him. Over there. That tall man in the doorway. I knew it. Let's go.'

I saw him. He was slouched, holding his collar up. When he caught us looking, he lowered his head and stared at the pavement in front of him.

Something broke in me: the happiness of this woman who'd loved me through all the idiocies I'd perpetrated on others was threatened by this creature opposite, staring at the pavement as if he didn't know or care that we were there, when all the time his eyes were on her. Always her. This madman was enjoying himself. I strode towards him and stood.

'*Pardon?*' he said. '*Quoi?*'

'*Qui êtes vous?*' I stammered.

'Are you English?' he said, ' English would be preferable, if you don't mind.' His politeness threw me. He wasn't French – he was English. Marjorie hadn't said that.

'Scottish, actually. Leave her alone.' I motioned Marjorie over my shoulder. 'She's my aunt. She's told me the whole story. I'm warning you. You're not dealing with an old woman here – you're dealing with me.' If I sounded like some idiot from a badly written B-movie, blame the situation – not one I was faced with too often.

'I don't know what you're talking about. Yes, I saw you with Marjorie a moment ago. Are you enjoying your stay? Oh, I'm Simon, Simon Harris. My wife's a friend of Marjorie. We live close by.'

'I'm confused,' I said. 'She told me you've been stalking her. Are you in love with her?' He laughed but his eyes were serious. This man was in his fifties only.

'The very thought. No. Your aunt's not well. Her friends are afraid that she'll do something stupid. She's become very erratic in her behaviour. Estelle wants me to keep an eye on her till we can get someone in to help. I know this must be a shock to you, but you can see how she is.' He glanced over. 'By the way, she's gone.'

I looked over my shoulder. Marjorie had indeed gone.

'I have to tell you she's tried to throw herself off the balcony twice now. Once the maid intervened and the second time a passing policeman shouted to her and she disappeared inside. We've no knowledge of any relatives so sectioning her was difficult without her permission. She's delusional. She imagines herself some latter-day princess to be adored by the world, yet in reality, it seems her money's almost gone. Estelle sees her once a week and manages to get some sense, but she's never mentioned you. We wondered who you were. When you appeared, we feared she'd negotiated some suicide pact or something.'

'I'm Eric Grieg. I'm her nephew. Christ, I'd no idea about all this. Last time I saw her, about a year ago, she seemed OK.'

'It comes and goes, the sense of who she is. But as time passes, the episodes of clarity get shorter. Look I'd invite you for a drink but my wife's upstairs at some ridiculous meeting of the Paris Sisters, and we're going to the opera tonight.'

I shook his hand and thanked him for his explanation. I told him that I'd stay longer and try to help her friends help her. We parted as the rain eased.

I went to the tree and looked about but there was no sign of her. The thought of returning to her apartment and going through her delusional stories again was too much for me so I continued walking towards Les Halles. I kept thinking of the gun and the need to get rid of it but the prospect of caring for her when her money ran out was a frightening one. It seemed so ironic that this woman, the shining beacon of her family for her lifestyle, wealth and charisma, should be on the edge of disintegration. As I strolled, deep in thought past the tourists with their infernal cameras, the tables salivating their threaded tin Eiffels, the wail of an ambulance rose like a wounded animal from the direction of the Sacre Coeur in the 18th arrondissement.

A LIFE IN CARPETS

1. Pattern.

"Angela - sweet, sweet, Angela. Where did it all begin, my love? You with your little legs tucked under your desk, me with my lustful thoughts. And that day when the motes swam down the sunbeams your legs crossed and that was us..."

'Well? How's that for an opening? Angela's you, Ellie. An angel. Get it? Falls away a bit but I think there's a touch of Donleavy about it don't you?' She looked at him blankly. It wasn't as if he expected a response. He knew she didn't read much. He knew she hadn't a clue who that Donthingy person was, yet somehow Bill liked reading out what he'd written each day when he should have been working. Thinks he's a writer but it's just gobbledygook, she thought, and all she wanted was intimacy, just a gentle word, a touch, and today something to herald the possibility that they may never see each other again.

'You know, Ellie, writers need a little encouragement. Just a word, a little nod, to acknowledge incipient genius.' The truth was, Bill saw Ellie less as an intellectual sounding-board than as a pair of spread legs and a flushed throat. He was Jean Paul Sartre but she failed miserably as Simone de Beauvoir. She was essentially a stupid girl who by chance had found herself sitting at the desk opposite him in the office of Mair's Carpets. She had swum into his world, her knickers in the air and her head down a toilet bowl. A staff night out. It was love at first sight. She was pissed and he was a steadying hand. Her gratitude knew no bounds that he could ever fathom.

Bill Goodman's little Nissan is parked by a pinewood play area. It is five forty-three p.m.

'I don't want you to go Billy. I've got used to you being there every day. I just know you'll never ring after you go.'

'I will. Of course, I will. It'll be different, that's all. We'll still see each other.' Bill pulls her to him.

'Don't Bill. I'm not in the mood now.'

'Christ, Ellie. I've never seen you like this. I only want to touch you.'

Ellie was married to an 'arsehole' and Bill conjured up 'frigid' for his wife. The pieces fitted perfectly for both sides. A perfect square. There should be a name for this, Bill thought, some Euclidian sexual theorem which only infidelity could solve. No, perhaps it was more like a square dance without the music. It wasn't that he didn't care for his wife, Sue, but a man, as everyone knows, has needs, and Sue's were a touch less carnal than his. Ellie was up for some fun she said, in the way many young people seemed to be up for things, and Bill, God knows, was up for her. Oh, of course, he was REALLY MUCH TOO OLD for her, she'd protest, at moments when it seemed as if the body and the tongue were not reading from the same hymn-sheet.

'I don't think I can face tomorrow night, Bill.' He looked at her dark hair as she turned from him, stroked it and then turned the key in the ignition. He would drop her at the end of her street.

2. Hard Wearing.

Bill was sixty-five and about to retire from "a life in carpets" as he liked to put it in his more sardonic moments. When they could, he and Ellie would go somewhere and make love: sometimes in the woods where they'd lie on an orange rug he'd been given by a traveller for getting an order. They had a favourite spot far enough from the path on a bed of needles (as comfy as an Axminster, Bill thought) so that no-one would see them and yet with the added thrill of hearing voices and barking dogs as their congress continued. Today though was the last time.

Tomorrow, he would no longer be an employee of Mair's Carpets. Alternative arrangements would have to be made. Thirty-five years at the same desk had shrunk to this. Like a pencil worn to a stub, his age had rendered him useless. He thought of the years when he'd climb out of bed at six-thirty on a freezing winter morning and drive the thirty miles to the office: of sitting there at his desk watching Harry picking his nose and flicking it on the floor; of the shish of Ellie crossing her legs as she became bored just before bun-break; of those tight days when he would wait to be "appraised" by old man Grant ('more of a friendly chat than anything, Bill') and later his son, Johnny, the baldy little idiot who would lean back and tap his pen as if he were tapping nails into your coffin ('more of an assault on the ego, than anything, Goodman').

After the old man went, it was downhill all the way. A rollicking downhill ride for Bill's increasingly shaky confidence as the mistakes piled up. It was as if his brain had decided it didn't care about carpets anymore. No matter how hard Bill tried to get things right, they went wrong, as the Goodman machinery broke down. Technology kicked in and with it the seasons of despair. Mair's Carpets - that was his life. Carpets! A building like a third rate motel in the middle of an industrial estate at the edge of a town. An overheated box attached to a warehouse had been his world. And strangely he'd been happy. Until young Grant appeared. Grant and a late blossoming realisation of a life gone threadbare.

A Life in Carpets

3. Colours.

'I suppose I should wear a tie for once. Oh God, I've only got three left - my black one, that one Meg gave me after she came back from Italy with God reaching out to Adam and this green spotted thing which I hate.'

'I like your green one, it matches your glass eye.' said Sue.

'Oh, hilarious.'

Sue was sitting at the dressing table doing her hair. She'd nice hair, he thought, for a woman her age, but she cut it too short now. He remembered hearing her mother's voice telling him how Sue's hair would go a very nice grey when she got older. Sue was in communion with her mirror.

'She's cut it too short. I should have asked for Anne.' She turned as he bent to brush a speck of shaving foam from his shoe, and asked if he was nearly ready.

'I'm not looking forward to this one bit' he said. 'I told them I didn't want a "do" but when did they ever listen to me.' She'd heard this so often in the last few days that she decided to ignore his whingeing. She opened her hands as if indicating the length of a fish she'd caught and pushed them into the neck of her dress. She placed it over her head and let it fall like a curtain on a performance. It slipped down her slim frame and she was red. From the toilet, she could hear his thin dribble as he relieved himself again.

'I've peed enough to float a boat today. Must be nerves.'

'There's nothing to be nervous about. You know them all don't you? Just relax and enjoy the night. They all want you to have a good time. Don't you think it's too short?'

'I know all that, but it's the speech I'm worried about. I've been thinking about it for ages and each time I try to remember it, I forget a new bit.'

'You've got notes. It's not a test of memory Bill. Well?'

'Well, I'll keep it short. Make a joke about short men and short speeches… What? Oh no, your hair's nice.'

'Do that. I'm not convinced.'

4. Fitting.

They arrived at the old coaching-inn that had been taken over a couple of years before and tarted up. It had been whitewashed outside and two big bushes in pots guarded the entrance like a pair of chesty bouncers. Inside, the shabbiness lurked like a stain that wouldn't go. He'd spent many evenings in the bar here and he recognised the old sporting prints with foxed mounts; the scratched paintwork where chairs had been pushed carelessly back; the stains of spilt beer crusted on the carpet and light fittings that had been known to shed fluff onto a pint when the fans came on. He was greeted by a chorus from three of his workmates at the bar as they noticed him enter.

'Here's the man!' they chorused, and he felt a quiver run through him. He was the main character in this little play, and he should know his lines.

'Well, you lot don't waste time, do you! The Belle of the Ball's just arrived and you're drinking the place dry.' It wasn't first class scriptwriting but he delivered the line with a certain elan which seemed to carry it. He introduced Sue and they were given drinks. As they chatted, other colleagues trooped in, smiling at Bill and nodding. The occasion had conferred on him some phoney status as a man to be reckoned with. He'd seen this film before and hated the predictability of the plot: the ritual celebration of every old fart who'd probably been a millstone round the firm's neck for years and whose special day had come at last to give them all a break. You had to be there. It was the done thing, no matter how little you cared for the central character. Bill felt awkward and angry that he was being acceded to because of his temporary and fleeting status. Some of these smiling faces hardly bothered to

A Life in Carpets

speak to him at work. I'm about to be retired he thought, ushered through a door into some unknown land. He had a vision of a horse being pushed into a horsebox, its legs stiff and angled against the frets of the ramp. No, he wasn't fighting this, but he could feel the press of hands on his flanks.

Sue was in conversation with a woman he didn't know and the talk around him was turning to football and the local team's failings. He couldn't see Ellie, thank God. As his hands felt the cool of another glass, his eyes strayed to a picture behind the bar of two men holding a huge fish in some Highland setting. That'll be me soon, he thought, as he felt a hand on his shoulder.

'You turned up then. I thought you might just stay at home, you bastard.' It was young Grant, his forehead shiny in the light from the bar.

'Shall we go through to the function suite? My God, I just called you "sweet" - see how much you mean to me?' There was a chorus of laughter from nearby and the group made its way along the corridor past harassed-looking fifteen-year-olds carrying trays and jugs of water. That was another thing about this place, Bill thought, the staff were just school kids who didn't know a thing about service but who were cheap. He saw in a flash the scuffed doors and dull paint of his dying father's hospital ward: no place to die in and this no place to retire from. He was aware of Sue at his shoulder, and when he met her eyes she winked. He knew it meant "Keep it up you're doing fine," and he knew he could keep it up for he'd found the rhythm of jokes and looks that would carry him through.

The head table sat eight, among whom were the Grants (old man Grant had died, but his wife Vi was here with her stick), the manager and his wife and Bill's buddy, Fox. Grant gave his spiel about what loyal service Bill had given the firm and how he didn't want to make this speech for he knew Bill would have liked to have been given a send-off by the man he'd worked for for twenty years.

Spoons were drummed on mats of Highland cattle, glasses raised to the dead. There were the usual jokes about the things you find in carpets; devious little mites and skin and hairs and how you can't always brush them under. Bill thought of Ellie and wondered if Grant knew. Grant smoothed his hand over his bald head as he did when he was feeling important and toasted Bill's future years. Everyone clapped heartily and settled back for Bill's speech.

Bill felt his hands shaking as faces turned to him at the table. He rose and glanced round. Old Vi seemed to be asleep, her head down on her chest, when he saw Grant's wife give her a tap on the shoulder and lean closer. As Bill drew breath to begin, he heard Mrs Grant's voice saying 'Johnny! She's not right!' Bill looked down at the crumpled paper in his hand and turned to see Vi being lifted from her chair by her son and Fox. A surge of relief swept over him, quickly replaced by the need to say something.

'Ladies and gentlemen, Mrs Grant seems to be unwell. I think we should attend to her before anything else.' There was consternation on the faces in the room as Johnny carried the old woman out. Sue pulled Bill down into his seat and told him to go and see if Vi was okay. He made his way along the corridor followed by some other diners and was met by Fox whose head was shaking.

'She's had it, Bill. They're trying to resuscitate her. There was a medical student at the bar. It doesn't look good though.'

'Jesus, what a thing to happen,' was all that Bill could say. 'We should call it off now. No-one's going to be in the mood for speeches now, are they?'

'You're right. Let's just wait a short time and then decide. We should take our lead from Johnny - it's his mother after all.'

5. Grip Strip.

Grant told everyone to go back in and have a drink and some did. Others wished Bill all the best and made their way solemnly out through the bar. Vi had been taken to a small side room, and the ambulance was on its way. As Bill looked round for Sue, a hand pinched his right buttock and he turned to see Ellie with that wicked look that vodka summoned.

'God what a terrible thing to happen, Bill. Hope she'll be okay.'

'I think she's gone' he said. 'Where have you been? I didn't see you earlier.'

'I was avoiding you. Didn't want to make you even more nervous did I?'

'You're all heart Ellie.' She bent towards his ear and said she'd found an empty room upstairs.

'You're joking! Sue's around somewhere.'

'It would be the first time in a bed, Bill. Just a quickie for your leaving present.'

She pulled him towards the stairs and to avoid being seen to be in a tug of war with one of the guests, he allowed himself to be steered upwards. On the first floor she pushed open the door to room 104 and they slipped in.

'Sue will wonder…' His protests were smothered by the lips of the panting Ellie who began to pull off his jacket while clutching his groin in a vice-like grip.

6. Laying Out.

The manager of The Coach and Pear (some sign-writer's incompetence that was treasured) was summoned, and concerned that his bar might empty in the presence of death, tapped lightly on the door of the ante-room where a red-faced young medical student (hauled from his Guinness by a foolish flush of professional pride) bent over a lady's corpse vainly trying to blow life into it. Occasionally he would straddle her and do a two-handed pumping action where he thought her heart should be. Grant and one of his friends watched ashen-faced with the same mixture of vain hope and yet probable despair one experiences watching a mechanic trying to fix a sick car. At length, exhausted, the young man stood up and shook his head. The big-end had gone, or rather, come.

'It's OK, you did your best,' muttered Grant and touched the chap on the shoulder in gratitude. As the student left, the manager put his head round the door.

'Sorry to intrude gentlemen, but I'm the manager.' He looked at the corpse and then at Grant to ascertain her condition. Grant shook his head.

'I'm really sorry. I was wondering if you'd like a bit more privacy upstairs. It doesn't seem right that she should lie here next to the bar.'

After a moment's thought, Grant agreed and lifted his mother.

'Put that round her Gordon, and we'll make this as quick as we can.' Fox did as he was told.

Grant lifted his mother, draped in the only piece of cloth they could find - an enormous Saltire flag stored for duty at televised games. 'What the hell,' he thought, and carried her through the bar which was practically empty now, along a corridor and up the stairs, preceded by the manager.

'104 should be OK" the manager whispered over his shoulder as Grant struggled to keep his feet through the trailing folds of blue and white. But 104 was locked when he tried it.

'Damn. Sorry, not the time for such language. I'll get the key.'

The manager flew down the stairs and Grant squatted by the door, his mother growing heavier by the second.

7. Underlay.

Ellie moved as she never had before, her hips gyrating to the slow rhythm of a jazz tune picked up from the next room, while under her, his trousers and pants dangling from his left leg, Bill lay at her mercy. His shirt, which she'd filleted like a fish, exposed a hairless chest which she would bend to lick now and again. As she began to make those little squeaky sounds that had always made him feel so good, he fought to keep his head out of things but failed miserably. The light from under the door flickered as if someone was there. Then he heard the rumble of voices. He glanced up at Ellie about to tell her that he couldn't really do this here when the sound of a key turning in the lock froze them both. Ellie pulled up the counterpane and her legs clasped him like a vice as the door opened.

8. The Bill (with the help of a Grant).

What the manager saw was a blue satin mountain as the beast- with- two- backs was stilled. Bill's balding head emerged to explain that the room was occupied and the door closed quickly. The manager's initial confusion soon turned to anger as he realised what was happening. He pulled the door shut again and turned to Grant, who was now standing with his mother in his arms ready to enter the room.

'I think we've got a bit of a problem.' muttered the manager, his face reddening. 'It seems the room is occupied after all. But it bloody well shouldn't be. Excuse me a moment and I'll see to this.' He disappeared to check the register again, convinced that some scam was taking place.

Grant slumped down with his mother and cursed the whole business, aware that a small stockinged foot was protruding from the folds. Fox stood wondering what he could do.

Inside the room, Bill unscrambled himself from the cover and from Ellie whose hair had turned her into a sobbing Medusa. She was frantically searching for her panties.

'Christ Almighty Ellie, you said it was free!' Bill yanked up his reluctant trousers.

Ellie's rear end did not reply but she continued to sob, scrambling to her feet to find her shoes.

'How are we supposed to go out here with half the office watching?' snapped Bill, who by this time saw in Ellie nemesis incarnate; the worldly flesh that had trapped him and was about to ruin him: a life of lies and half-truths grown wings and come together in the slight form of this stupid creature who by now was at the sink taming her mad hair. He threw off the covers and dressed hastily, tucking his shirt into his trousers. A knock at the door. A peremptory knock. Bill's shirt was fighting back.

'Shit. Just a moment!'

The door opened and the manager's head poked round.

'Sorry, but this room is not booked. I don't know what's going on, but I'm the manager here and I'd like an explanation.'

'My wife was unwell. She needed to lie down.' Sometimes the tongue takes leave of the senses in a way which leaves the senses gasping. To pretend that Ellie was his wife might have been sensible had his real wife not been less than hearty spit away and there was no way that Bill was going far from this room without his wife appearing. It was not a wise thing to say and Ellie's eyes, yes even simple Ellie, knew the folly of Bill's lie.

There was nothing for it but to go to the door and confront the manager.

Bill opened the door fully and saw a still startled Fox standing there in the dim light. To his right on bended knee was Grant clutching a Saltire from which a lock of grey hair fell limply.

'Bill!' gasped Fox.

'Bill!' repeated Grant, but with an edge of disbelief that threatened further discussion.

'My wife was unwell. We came up here to let her recover.'

'But Sue's at the bottom of the stairs. She was looking for you. Quite upset that you'd gone home or something,' interjected Grant, while something akin to enlightenment crossed his features.

'Ah," said Bill, having recovered from the diktat of the tongue in favour of the brain. 'Well, it's a bit complicated to explain.'

'Look,' said Fox, torn between a feeling of betrayal and of loyalty to his friend. 'Why don't we take Vi into the room and then we can go downstairs for a drink.'

'Just give me a minute then.' Bill pushed the door closed against the dull black shoes of the manager. 'Won't be long.'

The door closed and Bill turned. Ellie was sitting on the bed, her head in her hands.

'What can we do, Bill?'

'Let's go out calmly. Just go down the stairs as if nothing has happened, OK? You weren't feeling well, I brought you up here, and that's all there is to it.'

'But they saw us on the bed. They'll know something was going on.'

'Just the manager. I'll have a word with him. I'm sure he didn't tell the others what he saw. Anyway, there's nothing else we can do but brazen it out. Come on. Let's go down.'

Ellie opened the door and edged out followed by Bill. They didn't look at the others but calmly made their way down the stairs past the bemused trio. To their relief, there was no-one at the foot of the stairs. Bill told Ellie to go home and he'd phone her. She nodded.

The bar was by now almost empty of customers. In one corner he spotted three of his workmates who nodded to him as he ordered a gin and tonic. A woman he had never seen before came across and put her hand on his arm.

'What a terrible thing to happen on your big night,' she said, 'I hear Vi has passed away. Isn't that awful.'

'Oh, it's dreadful,' Bill echoed, glad to catch a mood which felt like an escape from the pursuing forces of guilt and retribution. 'Just awful,' he repeated. Then said it again. As Bill tipped his glass, he felt a hand on his shoulder and turned to see a red-faced Grant whose lips gradually thinned to what seemed like a smile.

He leaned close to Bill's right ear. 'You sly dog. You evil sly bastard. All this time I took you for a waste-of-space-washed-up old fart who couldn't cut an invoice and lo and behold all this time you've been screwing the lovely Ellie.'

'Ellie? No way. She and I are good friends that's all. You shouldn't…'

'Look, Bill, I've just lost my mother, remember? I'm not the happiest man in the world tonight. Even though the old trout was eighty-seven, it hits you, you know. So don't insult my intelligence. Not tonight, please. Now what will you have?'

Bill had another gin - a double and was about to finish it when Sue appeared.

'Bill. Where on earth have you been? I've been looking for you all over.'

'He was helping me with Vi, Sue, Grant chipped in. We put her in a room upstairs. Couldn't have managed without him. What a night, eh Bill. We won't forget this farewell in a long time, will we? Might have to do a rerun old son. Only right.'

Sue slipped her arm through Bill's and kissed his cheek.

'I'm not sure he'd like to go through all this again,' she said, and Bill smiled, raising his glass in agreement.

MAN SEEKS REASONABLE WOMAN

Sandra died a while ago but I still had Bob. Then two weeks ago Bob died after eating a chicken bone. The vet gave me his ashes in a plastic bag for he knew how I loved that wee dog. He said he didn't generally give folk ashes, but he'd make an exception for me. I went round next day and gave the receptionist a bottle of Glenfiddich for the man. She wasn't keen to take it but I persisted. Christ, you've got to give folk credit when they push the boat out for you. Anyhow, I put them in a wee box that Sandra bought at a charity shop years ago. It's shiny brown wood with a green glass inset on the top. Nice wee box for a nice wee dog.

'Poor bastard,' I can hear you saying. You're thinking I'm a poor old bastard that's got zero in his life but memories and a wee brown box with a dog in it. Well, you'd be wide of the mark if that was your conclusion. I won't deny its death was a blow, it was, but life goes on, and that includes mine. Anyhow, I've got my allotment and a wee bit grass out the back to keep me busy. The roses are smashing and in the good weather when it's not chucking it down, I like to sit outside and read the paper or a book. Christ the number of folk that can't believe a man like me would want to read a book. Well, that's always been a problem with me - not having an education. I left the school at fifteen and entered the wonderful world of work. Got my hands dirty every day and didn't leave with an occupational pension to feather my mattress. But a couple of years ago, I was lucky enough to end up in the same team as Willie Johnston one quiz night at the pub. What a guy!

If you were in his team, you had a winning ticket. Great brain, Willie, though he didn't ram it down your throat like some of them. Never looked down on you, Willie. Well, he gave me a new start.

I'd bump into Willie in the pub, and we'd have these grand discussions about the world. He was a teacher then, and he was always looking for pupils, if you know what I mean. No idea how it happened but we got in tow and became pals. He'd come over here, and Sandra'd be all smiles and make some soup, and we'd just sit and talk all night. Christ, come to think of it now, Sandra'd always rant and rave about my fads. Well, that was her word for any idea I had that she didn't understand. 'Can you not just accept life for what it is John. You're always fighting things.' Yet there she was, happy to see Willie and me gabbing away. Christ that man had a way with women right enough. She'd go to bed and there we'd be across the table having an argument about anything that moved. He gave me books that I'd never heard of: Steinbeck and Golding and Orwell, those guys. I loved them. I'd be sweltering near the furnace and in my head I'd be wondering what the Joad's next calamity would be. Got me going about politics and the class struggle too. Sitting there watching coppers belting Scargill's miners on the head while that Thatcher woman sorted out the working class. I got angry then, but you know, I'm not angry now. Oh, it's not because I don't care, far from it, but I've developed a philosophy that can be summed up in two words: things happen. There. You may think that's a bit simple, but when you look at the things people do and you reduce it to its simplest terms, you come up with simple truths. You can't stop things happening and when they do it's best not to panic. Sit back and wait, because if one thing's certain, it's that things will always work out. I've seen killers stop killing; bombers stop bombing; fat folk that couldn't move made thin and mobile again. I've seen the impossible made possible: the unstoppable stopped; the unprintable printed;

I've even heard Joyce next door having sex. Christ, what conclusion can you come to about folk and what they do: people make things happen, and people clear up the mess. Is the world going down the tube? Nope. And the Jehova's with their 'Isn't the world a terrible place and getting worse every day' routine. Pure dross. I used to get angry with Sandra when she'd let them in. Crows, that's what they are, I'd say: pecking misery out of anything good, but she didn't want to know what I thought by that stage. She'd gone all religious with Jesus this and Jesus that. It was like living with a nun. But you couldn't discuss any of it. No. So I suppose we settled for silence. Then she died.

Well, when Bob went too I thought about another dog, but I couldn't face getting used to it. I'd always be comparing it with Bob, and that wouldn't be fair. Mind you, can't deny I'm lonely since Sandra passed. Books aren't everything.

Oh, I can fill my days, but you can fill anything, it's what you fill it with that matters. Just feel lately that I'm not putting anything worthwhile into my days. Willie was all for me joining the bowling club. Christ sake man. I haven't got a beige jacket to my name so that's out.

So…big breath here… I decided to try my hand at dating. Ah can still hear Willie when I told him first. He looked at me as if I was daft. What are you thinking about, you're an old man for God's sake. Get another dog or a budgie or something sensible. A woman? Are you mad? I know Sandra was a good wife to you, but you'd have to start again, form a relationship for God's sake. Don't be daft John. Have another drink and forget it.

That was Willie: Willie the intellectual; Willie my friend and mentor all these years; Willie, who understands me and cares about me. And that was his response. Thanks, compadre.

Just when I needed a wee bit of understanding, just an ear to listen to me in my distress, I got nothing. Nothing. A budgie! What would I do with a bloody budgie? Would a budgie make me a cup of tea when I get back from the library? Would a budgie stroke my head when it's sore or go on holiday with me to somewhere sunny? Or maybe the upkeep of the wee creature would fill those lonely hours. I could heat up some porridge for it of a morning with a drop of milk and some nice wee seeds sprinkled on top. I could craft a wee chair and table for it to sit at. I could knit a wee pullover for it in the winter when it's freezing in here at night or clean out its cage every day, polish its wee mirror till it sparkled. I could talk to it about literature and teach the wee bugger to read. Today my little friend I'd like you to read James Lee Burke, and I'd like it read in a suitable Louisiana accent. No bother. What a terrific idea Willie - a budgie. Just what the doctor ordered.

No. I needed a woman. I told Willie not to judge all women by his own experience. I didn't impugn the virtues of the esteemed Mrs Johnston but to be honest, I'd rather sleep with a werewolf than sleep with her every night and him not a bad looking man too. I just wanted a nice woman. She didn't have to look like Marilyn Monroe or have the intellect of Helena Kennedy, but I was looking for something "reasonable."

The paper's a laugh. All those adverts in the "Women Seeking Men" bit. There're loads of lonely women in the world but most are not in their sixties. When you get to the older ones you're into supernatural territory, if you get my drift. Witches my friend. Hairs on chin jobs. Dewlaps too. I don't want a woman with dewlaps to rival your average bloodhound.

So this was it. This is one I made earlier, as Delia would say:

Gentleman, mid-sixties, fit, enjoys reading, moderate drinking, hates budgies, wltm reasonable woman of similar age and interests for companionship and more.

Most of them write "and more." I suppose it's a wee come-on for the boys. Anyhow, I wouldn't want to rule out sex altogether though the old prostate's not what it was.

So I put it in. Four days later I got two replies;

Dear Sir,

I read your advertisement with interest. I am a woman of sixty-seven. I enjoy reading and theatre and walking and have no interest in budgies. I liked your budgie bit - I thought that showed a rare sense of humour. I should tell you that I am mildly incapacitated and require a wheelchair some days when walking becomes hard, but I'm certain a man like you would not be put off by such considerations. The chair is of the very latest design and is just like pushing a light pram I'm told. I looked for a photo but couldn't find one that did me justice. Aren't we women vain?

Look forward to hearing from you. Keep killing the budgies.

Regards,

Linda McKechnie

She couldn't find a photo! Ha! "a rare sense of humour," she writes.

I wondered about the budgie bit. To be honest, that was Willie's idea. He came round to my way of thinking and really threw himself into the fight. 'You need to stand out,' he said, 'Make yourself different somehow.' And then he suggested using my budgie tirade. Well done Willie you've come up trumps again. Well, sort of...

Linda my dear, you're going to have to find somebody else to wheel you about. I don't care if you're sex on wheels - it's the wheels that bother me. Nothing against the incapacitated, not in the least, but I had an accident a while back, and I couldn't push drugs let alone a wheelchair.

The second letter was a laugh. It was an old dear of "over seventy" as she cryptically put it, who enjoyed the usual stuff plus spending long hours with her geraniums. Fair do's, she sent a photo, and she looked nice, but as Willie said, when was that taken? That's never a woman in her seventies in a million years. He agreed it was a bit of a risk, and she lived in the wilds so I should hang on for something better.

Well, I didn't get any more replies. You remember what I said about my philosophy
"Things happen." Well, a thing has happened.

I was in the library on Tuesday. It was pissing down outside, rain bouncing off the roof and me soaked and steaming. I'd taken back an Elmore Leonard Western and a James Kelman that I hated when the woman at the desk looked up and said 'Better than budgies then?' You could've knocked me down with a feather. Here's me going through the usual routine just itching to get among the shelves for something else by Leonard and this lovely blonde woman comes out with this budgie stuff. I smiled at her and wandered off to find some books. There was the usual detritus at the tables pretending to read papers and an old guy sleeping on a chair beside the foreign language tapes. Smelled like a toilet within twenty feet of him but what can you do? Libraries are for us all, I tell myself. Anyway, I can't get this woman's words out of my head and as I plonk myself down in a comfy chair to read "Valdez is Coming" I can hear her voice at the counter chirping away about what a miserable summer it's been. I get my book stamped and try to avoid eye contact. I'm pretty shy with women really and I'm out that door like a dose of salts.

Back home, I try to work out why she said that, and then I think she must like me. And then I think of Willie. He must've told the dragon about my advert. I'm on the phone to him, and he's all cagey, and then he says he told his wife and her friend works in the library. I was angry that it had got out, but a bit of me was excited too. She was a good-looking woman right enough, and I decided to just put it down to things happening. Here's me looking for a nice woman and here's one under my nose all the time.

I wrote a wee note asking if she'd like to go for a coffee sometime and I left it in a book sticking out so she'd notice. I put my number on for her to phone, and I did a wee drawing of me reading, with a caption saying "John: the keen reader and budgie lover." I thought the colon might impress her.

A week later I hadn't had any calls. I phoned Willie again and asked him about her, and he said she was married to a lawyer guy with money to burn. She works in the library because she's bored at home. Well, I was mortified. What a chump! I haven't been too well lately, and now it's back to square one. Sandra was a real gem when I was ill, I'll say that for her. I'm still keen on some company though, so I might just keep trying the paper or maybe go to one of these internet sites if I can learn to work our computer. Sandra was terrific on the computer. Willie says it's maybe the "reasonable" that's putting them off. Maybe "unreasonable" would be better. Me? I'm at a loss. Meantime it's just me and my wee box that glows when you look at it. And you won't believe this: when I looked closer at the box the other day, I discovered it had a wee bird in the middle of the lid - a wee green bird like a budgie. Would you believe it.

ASHES

It turned out his mother was in the safe. The guy with the pin-striped trousers, the jumpy one, looked as if he expected to be battered any minute. He'd been grabbing a smoke between ceremonies, and now this character had appeared wanting some ashes. He wasn't happy. He sat down at the desk, lifted a bit of paper and tried to look busy.

'We were told the funeral parlour would collect the remains of the deceased.'

'The remains of the deceased,' echoed Mac, 'The remains of the deceased are my mum, chum. I want her.'

'I appreciate this is a difficult time for you Mr…'

'McGuiness. Naw, it's no a difficult time. Ah couldnae stand the auld cow, but ah promised my brother I'd get her ashes and scatter them.'

'Do you have some identification?'

'Jesus.' Mac reached down into the inside pocket of his leather jacket and fished out a bank card and two condom sachets. 'That's me. Thomas Parnell McGuiness. OK?'

'You wouldn't have a utility bill by any chance. One with your name and address on it?'

'Nope.'

'Or a photograph with…'

'Nope.'

Through the window, a hearse appeared and made its slow way down the twisting drive. It was time Mr Funeral Man was on duty.

'OK. Sign here.' He opened the safe and handed Mac what looked like a brown shoebox.

Mac had left Boz in the car. When he got back, Boz had dozed off with his trainers across the driver's seat. "Motherwell are battling hard, but at two-down…" chirped the voice on the radio. Mac turned it down and shoved Boz into consciousness.

'Wha…'

'Right, my man. We have a passenger, so watch your language.'

'You got it then.'

'Yup. Easier without the box though.' He ripped open the box and extracted a dark plastic urn. 'Christ, it's like a fuckin Russian doll.'

He unscrewed the urn and found a plastic bag containing silvery ashes. 'We'll leave the urn and just take the bag eh? Now where'll we chuck her?'

They drove to The Crossroads Bar, downed a couple of pints then walked along the main street and up a lane which led to a small park. There were two kids on the swings, and their mothers were sitting nattering as Mac and Boz sauntered past. Afraid of dropping it, Mac carried the bag in the crook of his arm, a little baby close to his chest, soft and yielding, warming in the sun. Along a narrow road as far as they could from the swings and they were out of sight. Mac stopped, opened the bag and was about to throw the lot into a bush when a truck drew up with some council workers in luminous jackets. He clasped the bag to his chest, and the pair withdrew back down the road. He didn't need an audience.

'Shit. Just our luck eh Boz. Ma's about tae feed a wee tree when the green brigade turn up.'

'Och never mind. We'll find a nice quiet place.' As they made their way past the swings, Boz turned and asked if Mac's ma had ever taken him here. She had. Boz suggested that they get rid of some of the ashes by the play area which was deserted now.

'Give us a handful Mac.'

'What?'

'Give us a handful of yer ma. Did she enjoy flyin?'

'Never flown in her life, old son. Nae money for that lark.'

Without looking, Boz grabbed the bag.

'She'll fuckin fly now though,' said Boz, and he ambled across towards the deserted swings.

'Ah'll throw her when ah'm high if that's okay wi you Mac.'

'You're aye fuckin high, ya basturd. Go on then, gie her her first flight.'

As Boz was kicking out, gaining height, Mac had a sudden flash of memory. It was his mother in tears and screaming at his father who'd just told her they couldn't go to Benidorm after all because the fuzz wanted him down at the nick. His reverie was broken as Boz, clasping the bag with one arm crooked round the chain and swaying wildly, suddenly let out a shriek. His right thigh had cramped, and his face had turned into an impression of The Scream.

'Christ almighty, ah've got a fuckin cramp!' He stuck his leg out and swung like a dead weight losing height quickly. When the swing stopped, he sat and tried to bend back his foot with his free hand but lost his balance and fell backwards. The bag went flying.

'What are you doin, ya neep! You've just spilt her all over the place.'

The black rubberised matting had gone a brownywhite and some had landed on his jacket.

Mac helped Boz to his feet. By now the leg had begun to return to normal but there was still an echo of pain and Boz was not happy

'Christ that was sore, man! Ah'm stained with your mum now, Mac, but at least it's a start. There's a lot of her left, mind.'

They scooped handfuls from the ground and put them back in the torn bag. Mac didn't want to leave her here -

he wanted to scatter her somewhere more private. The thought surprised him. Sudden screams came from the path, and two small girls ran towards them. Mac turned.

'We're outa here!'

In the car they put the plastic bag in the box. Time for another pint. Mac insisted they take the box in with them. To his surprise, he was becoming proprietorial over the ashes. They had another pint with some salt and vinegar crisps.

Willie Dalgleish was playing pool with a bit of stuff in the back, and he noticed them and came through. He spotted the box.

'Boys. You been shopping Mac? Spect you're in the money now eh?'

'In what way exactly Willie?' Mac couldn't stand Willie. He'd been a pal of his at one time, but Willie had become a roofer with a family and bought his own home while Mac drifted along, a warrior against conformity as he saw it. Mac knew that Willie had come to speak to them so they'd register his bimbo at the pool table who was now leaning against it talking on her mobile and making faces. Giving Willie a hard time had become second nature to Mac now.

'Oh I just thought that with your mum dying and that, you might have inherited a few bob.'

'Willie you're a stupid fucker. Ma mum never had a penny. Fuckin funeral cost nearly two grand.'

'Just new shoes then,' said Willie, indicating the box.

'Aye, just new shoes. Ah think your wee friend's getting lonely through there. Why don't you go through and continue your discussion on the future of Neo-liberalism.'

'What? Oh aye, not bad eh? Teachin her a thing or two. Says she's aye liked ball games.' He winked. 'Well, see you guys.'

Boz watched Willie swagger towards Bimbo then turned to Mac.

Mac swallowed the last of his beer, flicked the mat in the air and missed it.

'Let's hoof it Boz.'

A pair of fuzz were chatting in the car park so they left the car at the pub and set off for Mac's house a few streets away, Mac clutching the box. Mac sniffed shit. He stopped and looked at his right sole then his left. Sure enough, he'd picked up some cack which now lodged squishy and yellow between the grey grooves of his boot.

'Fuckin dogs everywhere.' Boz had continued walking.

'Aye, bastardin things should wear fucking nappies or something.'

Boz was tall and thin with the stiff-limbed stride of a giraffe while Mac was small and stocky - a centre-forward of a guy who hated centre-halves, Boz the exception. Today they were moving from Myra's little flat to the Mac's family home, a two-up-two-down terraced property that once housed miners' families. Mac's father had been jailed for embezzlement from a High Street Bookmaker, and his battered Honda Civic had become a welcome set of wheels for his son. His brother was inside for assault with a deadly, and his mother had died of cirrhosis six days earlier. He hadn't gone to her funeral, but the bill had been taken care of by his uncle John, who loved his sister. Now the house was empty it would be a new adventure for the pair. Donna, his girlfriend, had shown him the door after months of threats. He had never really settled into family life, preferring the pool hall and the bookies to nights in with Noel Edmonds and Donna's hair-straightener. He'd miss his boy Stevie, who was four, but he wouldn't be far away. Boz had pleaded with Mac to let him move in and in the end, he'd agreed on condition that Boz didn't get in his hair or stink the place out with his trainers.

Turning the corner into Dungavel Street, Boz spat over a low wall into a garden. Bad timing. As the gob left his mouth a large man in a Gers top, who was more belly than man, emerged from a doorway and let rip at Boz.

'Fuck you think you're doin!'

Boz, not known for appeasement in these situations (and there had been many), rose to the bait of possible violence and stared at the man before voicing the word 'Turd'.

This would have been a prelude to a beating by Boz had The Belly not been joined by another two as frightening as the first. This was a triumvirate to be reckoned with and Mac began to fear possible annihilation. He patted Boz on the back and turned to the three who were now advancing down the weedy path.

'Guys, guys, this man isn't well. Can I have a wee word with you before we go any further…'

'What are you wantin - a doctor's appointment?' said Belly. 'What kind o' illness makes ye spit in folks gairdens - lawngitis?' At least the other two laughed which Mac took as a good sign, though he knew they weren't exactly home and dry yet.

'No, no it's more serious than that- it's cancer.'

'Your pals got cancer?' queried The Belly.

'Aye. Throat cancer. Phlegm builds up see. Needs tae keep spitting it out. Doctor tellt him.'

By now The Belly was a foot away from Mac. The latter could smell a waft of Tennent's Fifty-Shilling. Boz had come behind as if aggrieved that Mac was making peace when he wanted a go. The trouble with Boz was imagination. He had none. Didn't ever look beyond the moment. It just hadn't occurred to him that three beefy guys might beat him to a pulp. He hadn't looked a few minutes into the future to see himself being jumped on and his head become a football. He hadn't even thought of Mac helping him. He never did. Much to Mac's annoyance, he always ended up being battered in defence of his pal when he had played no part in causing the ruckus. Now as he faced The Belly, he realised he was on a knife edge. That one little word "turd" had done it. If only Boz could say 'Sorry chum' life would be so different, but now was not the time for such speculation.

'You, ya bastard, you spat on my gairden. What've you got to say for yersel?'

'He's sorry, really sorry, aren't you Boz.'

'No you, ya numbskull, him!'

'Say sorry Boz.'

Mac's plea over his shoulder elicited no response for what seemed a very long and dangerous time, till eventually a muffled 'Sorry.' emerged. To Mac it was like a soothing shower on a hot day. The word flowed by him and he hoped it would land somewhere sensitive.

'Awright. Now pick that up ya bastard.'

'What?' enquired Boz.

'Pick the fucking gob up. There it is, there on the grass.'

'That's not my gob,' said Boz, but before the words were out his mouth, Mac had louped the wall, crushing a daffodil on landing and scraped up the slime in his hand. He felt his stomach make some comment. Rarely had anything felt so disgusting, but rarely had the need for sacrifice been so pressing.

'Sorry about the daffy,' said Mac, 'Gents, as you can see, I've removed the offending gob which I will place in a handkerchief and dispose of in the nearest bin. If that's all gentlemen, we'll be on our way. And I'd like to thank you gentlemen for being so reasonable.'

Mac's words were oil on troubled waters. That silver tongue had done it again. The pair moved off aware of the three stares boring into their backs as they moved up the street. Boz started to speak but Mac told him to shut up. Just walk. 'Tell you something though, Boz old chum, that bastard's got a lawn full of dog-shit now.'

'You fuckin beauty!' said Boz, punching the air in delight.

Ashes

The house reeked of beer and urine but it was tidy. Mac hadn't been here in months. Every time he came within a hundred yards of his mother she turned into a snarling animal and he'd learned to keep away. It had all turned sour when he'd screwed his young cousin Vicky and got her pregnant. She'd been a favourite of his mothers and when it became obvious that Mac didn't give a damn about what he'd done, her old man had tried to batter him one night. When Donna became pregnant shortly after, it was too much for Mrs Mac to bear and she'd vowed to have nothing more to do with "the wee scumbag" as she called him.

Mac took off the offending boot and placed it outside the back door. He'd scrape the rest of the shit off later. He washed the slime and grass from his hand with a small hard green bar of soap, dried it on a towel, then placed the box containing the ashes in a cupboard.

The house was a memory heated up. Mac saw himself on the mantelpiece as a grinning twelve-year-old in his school tie and next to him his brother with one foot on the ball in the middle of a five-a-side team photo. He told Boz to have a look at the DVD's and wandered through to the kitchen. He opened the fridge which smelt like a swamp. In the bottom vegetable compartment, various green things were ganging up to produce something nasty. He closed the door.

Upstairs he went into his old bedroom and sat on the bottom bunk. The room was tidy apart from a pair of white sports socks that lay yellowed in one corner. The walls looked like they were covered in butterflies for old posters had all been torn down leaving only pinned corners as if his mother had had a fit of vengeance against her sons. Even the beds had been stripped and the Celtic rug lifted. His books were still there though - the Bukowski's that he'd loved and The Grapes of Wrath that he'd read at school for his Highers. At university, he'd read and read but when he left after a troubled year, he'd given his books to a pal in exchange for his fare home.

He wandered through to the other room and looked through a few drawers wondering if there might be some money lying hidden somewhere. In the bottom cupboard of his mother's bedside table, he spotted a small wooden box under a pink bed-jacket and some knitting. He took it out and opened it. It still smelled of cigars. At first, there seemed to be nothing but some old bills and buttons and an old bowling medal of his father's but then he noticed a small bundle of papers bound tight with a brittle green elastic band. He pinged it and rifled through what were letters. As he read them from his brother and himself to his parents, it was as if he were writing them again for the first time. He could see where he'd been when he wrote them and relived the feelings that had provoked them. He only ever really wanted things, he realised as he read… "If you could see your way to sending me… things are a bit tight money-wise at the moment…my wallet was stolen at the weekend and I don't know how I'll get enough for the train home…" Lies. All lies. He'd been skint all right but only because he'd gambled away every penny. He saw himself in the grotty flat near the slaughterhouse and could hear the slam of the bolt as the lights danced on the wall. There had been an outside toilet and one night, bending over the bowl to puke he'd flushed away his wallet with forty quid in it.

She'd kept these letters. Those from his brother when he'd been away down South working were all about how homesick he was and how he missed him mum's rhubarb tart and all that crap. His were cold and clutching, never showing any feelings though there were times when he did long for home and its safety. His hands shook as he read them and he put them back in the box. At the bottom among the rattle of buttons and badges, he found a piece of paper with a doll-like drawing of a woman with curly hair. "My mummy by Tommy" There was also a medal with his school badge which he'd won in a relay race. He realised his mum must have kept these things because they were part of his life. Something stirred in him.

Boz had found Taxi Driver which he hadn't seen for a few years he said.

'Cool fuckin dude Mac. Look what he's made for his arm…'

'Boz old son, I've changed my mind about the ashes. Ah owe her a bit of decency. Ah'm going to take her back to the cemetery and bury her properly with a wee stone or something when ah've got some dosh.' Boz was lying on the sofa, his trainers in a v-shape so that he could see the screen. Mac was suddenly angry and saw a future that appalled him.

'Feet off the sofa. Sit properly in the fuckin chair will you. Have a bit of respect.'

Back in The Crossroads that night, the pair fell in with a school friend of Mac's, Tam McShane, a sharp character who ran a builder's yard manned by two rather fierce German Shepherds. Tam knew Mac had had some success as a teenager competing on the go-kart circuit and told them he had a special job he needed help with. Tam's eyes had provided the emphasis for "special" - an audacious wink that told Boz and Mac all they needed to know about the legality of the proceedings. Boz was politely asked to take a walk while Tam outlined exactly where and how and when the operation was to take place. Mac was desperate for money. Mac was essentially honest. Mac needed money. Mac agreed, if Boz could come as back-up, just company really. Tam hesitated a moment then agreed on the understanding that the pair would only get one share.

Three nights later Mac drove slowly along a half-lit back street on a commercial estate. He was told to stop by a blue wooden door. In four minutes, Tam and his sidekick Grunt, both now balaclavad and breathing heavily, would return to the car which should be ready for the off. Mac looked at his watch but couldn't make out the time clearly in the dim light. Boz rubbed his hands gleefully and sang "We're in the money, we're in the money…"

'Wrong. I'm in the money. You're along for the ride chum.'

'Aye. Of course. I know that, Mac. Just happy for you. And your old mum and all that.'

'What's the time?' asked Mac.

'Ten to.'

'They've been away about a couple of minutes I reckon. Should be out any minute. The engine of the Jaguar purred contentedly. It was then that a car's headlights appeared in their rear-view mirror. A car slowly approaching them as if it was about to stop.

'Jesus. What's going on?' said Mac.

'What's wrong?' said Boz.

'A car. Stopping behind us. Could be the fuzz. Shit. Come on, Tam!'

The car had stopped about twenty feet behind Mac. The headlights were doused. Mac could feel sweat running down his side. The blue door remained closed. He looked at Boz, who was now turned staring at the car. Mac revved the engine in the hope that Tam might hear and get a move on. He imagined the pair emerging with their holdalls and getting into the car. He also imagined a couple of burly fuzz emerging at the same time. The blue door crashed open, and Tam emerged holding up the limping Grunt.

'Fucking idiot tripped and did his ankle. Cretin. Get a fucking move on. Now!'

'Look behind,' said Mac. 'Could be fuzz.'

'Shit. Drive. Just drive will you!' Tam was frantic.

Mac gunned the motor and they sped off swerving to avoid a man crossing the end of the street. They turned left at the lights and then a wide sweep took them onto the main road. Tam looked behind but there was no sign of any car following them. He relaxed and pulled off his balaclava. Grunt already had his off and was now moaning to himself.

'Shut up Grunt. We've done it, boys. Like taking candy from a baby.'

'How much you got anyway?' said Boz, who had opened his window for some air. At that moment, a snow of paper emerged from Grunt's side of the car. His bag had been open.

'Close the fucking window, you moron. We're losing half the dough. Jesus. Every fucking time I do a job, there's some moron that wrecks things.'

'OK Tam,' said Mac, 'Just take it easy. No need to be insulting.'

'What? Are you talking to me, McGuiness?'

'Are you talking to me?' said Boz in a very good imitation of Robert De Niro.

Tam slapped Boz on the back of the head and he yelled in pain.

'Stop the car Mac' said Boz.

'Can't Boz. We'll sort this out later. Keep calm.'

'Stop the car Mac. Now. Pull over.'

'Stop this fucking car and it's the last thing you do came Tam's voice from the back. This was enough for Mac. He drew to halt in a lay-by, switched off the ignition and opened his door

'Out.' He said, opening Tam's door.

'This is my fucking car, Mac. What do you think you're on?'

'Tell you what, Tam. Keep your fucking money and I'll keep better company, OK?'

Mac pulled Tam from the car and delivered a quick kick to his testicles. He doubled up and lay moaning.

'You too Grunt.'

'I can't walk. Ma ankle's bust.'

Boz had now emerged and always eager to emulate his hero Mac, delivered a swift kick to Grunt's good ankle. He screamed and crumpled.

'That'll even things up a bit. How about the money, Mac. These idiots don't deserve it.'

'No. They can keep their money. We'll leave them to it and walk back to town. Boz seemed rather puzzled by this plan but fell in with it. The pair began walking along the grass verge, buffeted by fast trucks on their way to the harbour. As they got closer to the town they began to come across £20 and £50 notes scattered in their path. They stuffed their pockets, crossing the road at one point to search for more.

At home, they counted their takings. Seven hundred and forty pounds.

'What about Tam, though?' said Boz, tipping a Becks down his neck. 'He'll be looking for us now.'

'No doubt about it, old son,' said Mac. 'But first, we give the old dear a decent send-off. You know Boz, I've just decided what I'll put on her stone.' He stood up and with his right arm in the air he wrote 'For mum from your loving scumbag.'

'Great idea,' said Boz.

MOTHER ICARUS

The postman had rung the bell. Shorts today. A big smile. Another registered letter. She must have seemed strange, half dressed, frowning, a plaster still on her head where the phone had struck. Mostly these days she'd just shut down, staring into space as if her mind needed the relief that nothingness brings. One mistake, just one mistake and now this. The children seemed afraid of her, had become quiet. When she looked at them, she wanted to pin those dear faces down before they floated away, for everything seemed to be going from her. She was closer to nothing herself now, falling. Earlier, with her hands in the sink's scalding water, it came back to her: that poem about Icarus; how life just went on while he plummeted. That's what she'd become – Icarus, plunging to earth while the world smiled. Smiles mocked her now.

She stayed away from work to look after Shona, the wee soul crying a lot and not to be comforted. The children believed her story that he'd gone to work away from home, only occasionally mentioning him when they wanted praise for something they'd done or they thought of somewhere he'd taken them once. In their childish selfishness, she saw the ultimate irony: that they needed him only for what he gave them.

Each day crushed up against the next, drawing her nearer the day he'd threatened. She knew their sweet smells would dissipate, the dust collect on shoes too small, the toys lie there discarded, the bright crazy cartoon duvets remain obscenely neat. She couldn't imagine loving them by the calendar. What kind of life was that? And what would become of her when the scaffolding collapsed, for it was only the kids that kept her upright? From the chaos of her imaginings however, a clarity came: a future that promised no pain. Slowly, with a shiver, the unthinkable visited her and stayed.

Now, as usual, she threw the letter in the wastebasket by the dressing table. Too many knife wounds. When Robert came in the blood was in her cheeks. He asked her what was wrong. She hugged him and brushed some jam from his mouth. The sun's heat was still in his hair. When he went downstairs, she knew finally and completely his warmth was too precious to lose.

She braved the mirror and brushed her hair. Under her eyes the bags were carrying bags. She looked hellish. For weeks she'd forgotten herself: sometimes didn't even shower, only brushed her hair when she remembered. Every day it was jeans and the first top she could find, losing any sense of herself in her anxiety over them. Today of all days, she'd put on that summer dress with the fruit motif. She'd always loved that dress. She took the photo of the kids as planned and slipped it into the deep pocket. Just so they'd know. In the bathroom, she made herself up for the first time in weeks, her hand shaking as she applied mascara. A quick glance in the mirror. Two paracetamols. She was ready.

Downstairs, she felt the sharp edge of her wedding ring bite when Shona took her hand. She hated the thing now, but they might notice if it went. She didn't want any more questions. Now it was Saturday and today they were all going on their picnic. The kids looked up from the cartoon they were watching.

'OK guys, it's picnic day. We'll walk up to the crag and have our picnic at the top.' They'd never been up The Crag. Shona ran off to put on a picnic frock with her usual need to dress for the occasion. Robert said couldn't he just play football, but when she said they'd have crisps and caramel wafers and she'd make ham and tomato sandwiches

Mother Icarus

with pickle, he nodded his head like that stupid bulldog in the car. Robert liked pickle – just like someone else she once knew. They'd have juice too. He asked if he could take his ball but she said it was too hilly so he should leave it at home. There were woods up there to play in, she said, they'd like it. She switched off the TV and pulled out the plug. Laughed to herself. She felt so calm today.

They took the bus to the centre of town and got off opposite the Chest, Heart and Stroke shop where Shona had got her coat. Robert pulled her up when he spotted a Rangers shirt in the window for four pounds and they bought it. He put it on over his t-shirt, proud as anything. Shona got a pink plastic handbag.

As they walked along the High Street towards the bridge, she felt stares. A mother holding the hands of her children. What was so strange? Was it her orange dress? Was it their picnic bag dangling from her wrist? It did knock her leg repeatedly but she ignored it. She kept up a good pace and bent to talk to each of them from time to time. She had never felt so balanced; one each side, striding on; never felt so clear about anything as she did this sunny day. She prayed they wouldn't meet anyone they knew. Not now. Not today, please God. No smiles today. No polite chat. They passed the sculpture of the two figures inside the hula-hoop and felt the sun's warmth come and go as the clouds passed. By the river, two gulls squabbled over a burger. They crossed the bridge. She wondered for a brief moment at the power she had now: at his helplessness. His face flickered in her brain. Robert wanted to be lifted to see the river but she hurried them on. Across and right and along another busy road of large Victorian houses whose lawns sloped down to the river. Some were old-folks' homes, and they could see old ladies through the windows sitting playing cards and having tea. One of them waved. Icarus is plummeting. Enjoy your game. At the end of the road, they crossed and began to climb a path which read "Devil's Crag Tourist Trail."

The path was red gravel and there was no-one about. Robert broke from her and ran ahead, then Shona as always, followed. Her instinct was to call them back but she kept silent. What did it matter. She stopped walking, stood stock still for a moment and the world stopped with her. The sun was on her head, pressing. Last things crowded her: today she washed her last dishes; this the last walk she would take with them; these birds the last she would hear. They seemed so cheerful. The day so cheerful as if it wished her well. Or did it mock her? Did the day know? She looked up and saw a speck hovering, then Robert calling,

'Mum, Shona's fallen.'

She'd tripped and grazed her knee on the path. Those little legs that couldn't keep up with her enthusiasm Why did children always run? Everywhere they run. Robert still ran, though less than he did. Do you slow when you learn that the world will wait? Do you slow when the world bites first? She held her till the sobbing stopped and looked at her as if willing the frown to become a smile. It did, as always. She was warm, hinted of toffee. Only a little scrape with the pin pricks of blood to remind her as the stinging receded. She wondered why the moment, the day, failed to quell her instincts. Why fuss about this now? They'd have their picnic at the top. She'd promised a picnic. A promise kept meant so much. She'd thought of some calming strategy before they did it, but the thought of drugging them appalled her. They'd find a nice grassy spot at the top not too far from the edge and they'd eat a last meal together.

At the top a family was sitting having their picnic and not far off a pair of young men were arguing as they battled with a hang-glider. It muttered in the wind. She wasn't bothered. She'd been here before and knew a dip where they wouldn't be seen.

'How about here?' she asked.

'No, it's too near the edge mum,' said Robert.

Mother Icarus

'It'll be fine. Just watch out, that's all.' The boy seemed puzzled at his mother's trust. She'd never before seemed to trust him near danger, always pulling him away from things with the tug of her warning voice. Now he absorbed the danger himself, almost proud of it, standing six feet from the edge of the Crag from where he could see for miles and miles. Cars sped along to the next city like scurrying bugs.

She spread out the tartan travelling rug and they delved into their sandwiches. She feigned eating but the sandwich had no taste and she felt her stomach rebel.

'These are the ones without pickle.' Robert squatting, one leg bent under him the way she used to sit when she was a teenager. She looked at him and that prickling feeling came to her cheeks that she knew would soon be tears. His hair flopped over his right eye and for a moment, she saw him eighteen and huge, his legs covering the rug, his handsome face lit by the joy of youth. She reached for his little hand and kissed it.

'Mum!' he shrank from her. Who could blame him? An unaccustomed gesture of love taking the boy by surprise after weeks of being without a mother or father. He had turned to Shona to see if she'd noticed, but she was busy chewing and placing crumbs in her new bag.

'What are you doing Shona?'

'It's for the birds.'

'Oh. Right.'

The juice was spilled as usual and formed self-contained blobs on the rug. She dabbed it up and wondered why she was doing it. Old habits. She stood up.

'Just finish your crisps. I'm going to look at something.'

'Can I come?' asks Robert.

'No. Stay with Shona. I won't be a minute.'

She made her way to the cliff edge by sliding down a steep bank between gorse bushes. As the land below spread out before her, she felt the wind nudge her hair. The warm air from the Strath rising to greet her. She flapped her arms. She was ready to fly. Now she was two feet from the edge and she became dizzy. She slumped back and lay looking up at the clouds which had gathered in a group and were slowly obliterating the sun. She'd always hated heights. That perverse pull that is the voice of oblivion calling. "Jump into the void. Fill the void with the loveliness of falling." So subtle. No matter the height, it called, even as a child scaling the climbing frame or a tree. With every foot up the voice gained strength. The ground wanted her to join it, to become one with it again – dust to dust. And it was as if the brain, the will, was in collusion. Why did she think she could do this? Yes. She could. It was for them. For them. She'd answer the call and she'd take them with her down and down into whatever lay in wait. Safe. For a moment, she imagined him picking up his phone. His face as he heard the news. It was the only way. She sat up, ran her fingers through her hair and scrambled back up.

Robert had found a stick and was poking at some ants. Shona had drifted across to the other family and was being offered a drink.

'Shona! Come here! Leave those people in peace.' Arms raised suggested there was no problem, a woman's glassy laugh, but the child turned and made her way back still holding a blue plastic cup filled with orange.

'I've found a place to explore. Just over there but you'll have to be brave. It's quite near the edge. We can see for miles. I'll point out Auntie Jean's farm. If we take each other's hands, we'll all be together.'

From the blue bus, only one pair of sleepy eyes witnessed but did not register a flutter of orange and blue and white against the red crags. Doreen Ogilvie was half-dozing in that sweet oblivion that is gifted the middle-aged. The sun had broken through and was suddenly hot through the glass, her magazine slipping from her lap. When she read the headline the next morning, she told her husband she'd passed the cliffs on her way home from visiting her daughter-in-law. What a terrible thing. But she'd just seen her new granddaughter for the first time and the world was kind, its gift pink and gurgling. She asked if he'd like more tea.

THE FLUTE

Kirsty was in her element in the house's bright, newly installed kitchen. Her own was small with ancient cheap pine cupboards which had a tendency to wobble when she opened them, but here, in the space between sink and fridge and Aga, she moved like a dancer. It was just a pity that every time Kirsty pirouetted, there would be the tall gangly figure of Klaus wanting to fill his flask and ask her questions, sometimes rather personal ones. She'd taken to telling him that curiosity killed the cat, but puzzling this one out only seemed to intrigue him further. Was there a German equivalent?

Klaus was there again today. She wondered what he wanted this time. Whatever it was, he wouldn't be able to find it and she'd have to break off and help him. She'd point to a teapot or a fruit basket which for some reason must have been invisible to him. Men, she thought: why can they never look properly? She just wanted to be left to get on with things in this sprawling country house where she was cooking for a group of hill-walking Germans. It was late in the season and the weather poor, but this tour, coinciding as it did with a local folk festival, had been fully booked. The group loved folk music, and David, the tour guide, played Dougie McLean's "Caledonia" interminably as the bus rolled its way north from Edinburgh. According to Elke, the genre had disappeared from their own country after the war, in the disavowal of all things essentially German. With a younger generation emerging however, old yearnings were stirred anew.

The Flute

So here he was Klaus again this morning, soon joined by his two old college friends, the lovely Monika and the rather shy, Elke. Kirsty was sure they'd giggled when they spotted Klaus hovering. Perhaps they'd decided he was more interested in her than he was in his tea. Ignore, she told herself.

When the kitchen was hers, Kirsty sighed and turned to the sink. She could hear the group booting up by the bus for the day's walk, as she set about preparing the roast, the potatoes and the carrots. She lingered for a moment by the dresser to catch the tail-end of a phone-in on the radio about reintroducing wolves to Scotland and laughed at the thought that one had already been introduced into her kitchen.

After an hour or so, assuring herself she was ahead of the game today, she'd explore the garden for the first time.

Set on a hillside, the garden at the rear was terraced to trap the warmth from a Southern exposure. It was out of season now, and the vegetable beds were bare, only clumps of sad sprouts and those huge crinkly-leafed things whose name she couldn't remember, left standing. Around the chunky bird-table, living on memories, a family of sparrows and some coal-tits flitted, while a huge crow perched on a pole seemed to be wondering what the commotion was about. She continued to zig-zag up the soggy wood-chipped path till she was looking down on the house which had shrunk surprisingly quickly as she climbed. A bench was grubby with twig litter so she stood for a moment and watched a helicopter drift above the valley whose dense pine forest clung like a dark garment. As she ambled down again, a movement caught her eye. She thought the figure coming round the house must be the postman at first but he'd called in his van the previous day and he'd been a small man – this man was tall and a little stooped and he seemed to be carrying a sack of some sort. He stopped and looked in the kitchen window then wandered round the house out of sight. She thought of calling but decided she was too far away to keep him waiting and he'd probably just leave any parcel in the vestibule at the front. This was the country after all and people didn't steal things here.

She took off her boots at the kitchen door, slipped on her flip-flops and clattered through to the hall. There was no mail in the basket. She opened the door but there was nothing in the vestibule either and no sign of the van or the postman. There wasn't even a little red card saying he'd tried to deliver a parcel as happened at home. Strange, she thought, but quickly forgot the whole business as there was still plenty to do before dinner that night.

Distracted by her thoughts, she cursed as her knife slipped and sliced her index finger. It was then that she heard the sound of music upstairs. She ran her finger under the tap and winced as the cut dribbled watery pink into the deep butler's sink. As she dabbed it dry and placed a blue plaster over it, she wondered what could have made the noise. There was no-one else in the house but her, as far as she knew. She needed to check. Perhaps a radio had come on. It did happen.

She made her way into the hall and looked up the stairwell. There were traces of mud on the first few steps which was very unusual, for the walkers always took their boots off before mounting the stairs. Then a sound came again; a thin tremulous note. A flute? She could feel her heart speeding as she mounted the stairs. Her legs had become heavy. Though she told herself not to be silly, her palm was sticking to the bannister. The sound was coming from room 6, at the end of the corridor. Klaus's room.

She knocked on the door and waited. The music continued. Tentatively, she opened the door, expecting to see Klaus, who must have returned from the walk for some reason. Sure enough, sitting on the bed, still in his boots, his head bowed, Klaus was playing on a wooden flute. He turned his head and glanced across at her then resumed playing. She'd never heard such a mournful tune but each

The Flute

note was pure and beautiful in the chilly air of the room. He didn't say anything. There was a strange blankness in his stare and his hair was flat and matted. Kirsty struggled to speak at first then murmured an apology. She closed the door, wondering why this normally chatty man now seemed so unfriendly. She stood there outside his room as the music faded then rose again and wondered if she should go back in and ask why he'd come back from his walk but something in her, perhaps the instinct of the pursued woman, told her to leave him be, particularly as he didn't seem very happy. She went downstairs again, relieved that she'd discovered the source of the music but still puzzled by his behaviour.

The clatter of saucepans was comforting, but between sounds the silence was palpable. The music had died and an eerie quiet settled like a pall on the house. She knew he was up there, that he'd seen her in his room, though he'd said nothing. Perhaps he'd come down, apologise. She poured out the dregs of her coffee and though she tried to remain calm, the image of Jack Nicholson in The Shining swam into her head. She saw him breaking down the door with the axe and that crazed grin as the wood splintered. What if Klaus had simply flipped in some way? What if he really did fancy her, was obsessed with her, for God's sake, and the giggles of the others had caused him to feel humiliated? What if he blamed her for leading him on? Men did that. You just had to be kind or make a joke and they would imagine you fancied them. What was he doing now? The more her mind raced, the more oppressive the kitchen and the house became. She had to get out.

She pulled her blue anorak from the hook and slipped out the kitchen door. It had started to rain, a thin drizzle that soon made her shoulder glisten. She touched her hair and pushed it behind her ears, something she always did when she was nervous. It would be ages before the group returned and she could feel safe, but she had a meal to prepare. She looked at her watch. Ten to twelve. If she got back by two, it would be time enough. But where to go?

She parked in the village and found a little bistro which offered some sanctuary from the rain. Celia ordered a coffee. The young girl asked if she'd like anything else, some chocolate cake? She declined, tapping her hips. The girl smiled. There were two elderly ladies, a couple of walkers who'd hung their steaming cagoules over their chairs and an old man with a Dachshund, which stared at her dolefully. All things German plague me today she mused and smiled at the old man when he looked up from his paper. She fiddled with her spoon when she heard the first rumble of thunder followed by a Hollywood rain lashing the windows. The young waitress moved to the door and peered out. A hiss of steam emanated from the kitchen in the rear, together with an expletive. The old man looked up and the dog rose stiffly. Kirsty thought of her group who had set off to climb a Munro five miles further up the valley. She imagined them exposed to this onslaught high up the side of the hill and suspected the walk would be aborted. She knew David would get them all back safely. She finished her coffee and paid the smiling blonde woman at the counter.

Sitting in her van, soaked from the short dash, as the windows steamed up, the thought of returning appalled her but it seemed that her options had run out. She had to go back. They would all be returning soon. Klaus could go hang himself if he was upset. It was no fault of hers whatever was up with him.

It took her ten minutes to get back to the house, and drawing up with a loud crish on the soggy gravel drive, she was astonished to see that the bus was already there. Kirsty couldn't believe it. How could it have arrived so quickly when the weather had only recently deteriorated? As she slammed the car door, David appeared. He was pale and obviously anxious.

The Flute

'Where've you been Kirsty? I tried your mobile. God, it's awful; it's Klaus.'

'Klaus? He's in the house. He came back. He was in his room playing a flute.'

David put his hands on her shoulders. 'What are you talking about? He's dead. He had a heart attack on the hill, just crumpled and lay there. No pulse. Dead. We took him to the hospital in the village. They're all in shock.'

The house, normally a cacophony of gushing bath-taps, crackling logs, slamming doors and laughter, had taken on the sombre quiet that catastrophe brings. The silence had shut doors and mouths, pushed people into themselves. Smiles became nods of acknowledgement as you passed someone in a corridor. Kirsty's kitchen, the warmth of which had been such an enticement, was avoided by those who had associated it with Klaus and his untimely visits. Kirsty, stunned and bewildered by the events of the day, forced herself to prepare the evening meal though she wondered who would eat it, her own stomach churning as she bent to the oven to remove the lamb. She sipped some water and its coolness seemed to help her concentrate for a time. She'd say no more to David just yet, leaving him to settle the collective grief as best he could, though she knew nothing like this had ever happened before on his tours.

At the meal, attended by less than half the group, David had called for a moment's silence to pay their respects to Klaus. Eyes were lowered for a short time till David tapped his plate lightly and urged them to eat, for he was sure Klaus would have been one of the first to 'dig in.' There was a brief flurry of laughter, and the quip seemed to have worked as dishes were passed round. Kirsty sat by Monika, who toyed with her food for a time before excusing herself and disappearing to her room. When the meal ended, Kirsty told David she had to talk to him urgently.

That night in her room, she told David about Klaus, the flute, the mud on the stairs, everything, and he listened patiently. He was obviously fatigued with the emotional responsibility that had fallen on him but he clasped her hand and agreed to a search of Klaus's room. They found nothing exceptional: no boots, no traces of mud and no flute in his belongings though there was the imprint of a weight on the duvet. She pointed to it, but David opened his arms in a gesture suggesting it meant nothing.

'Just sat there after he'd made his bed, Kirsty.' By now, doubts drifted through her mind like snowflakes. She had seen him, she had, but how was it possible? Nothing in her life had ever prepared her rational mind for such a phenomenon. She didn't even believe in ghosts for God's sake. There had to be an explanation but it would take her some time to work out her questions. They agreed to say nothing to the others. With two days left of the tour, it was agreed that guests could stay or go as they thought fit but even those who were staying moved like zombies.

The next morning some of the group had already gone and Kirsty was in the kitchen when Elke appeared, baggy-eyed and spent, asking for some tea. Kirsty knew that the girl wanted to talk.

'I'm so sorry Elke,' she said, hugging her. Still in the hug, Kirsty released the question that had made her night so long. She asked if Klaus could play the flute.

'Yes, he played with a group in college. Not very well.' She smiled. 'Why do you ask this?'

'Curiosity. That old cat again,' said Kirsty, turning, momentarily disorientated in the steam from the kettle.

FEARLAS MOR

I'll never forget that October. It was stuffy in the car going up and the kids were restless. "I Spy" didn't last long before squabbling broke out over whether "mountain" could begin with an "m." Judy, always a stickler for rules, maintained that mountains had names and you couldn't just point and say "mountain". James said he thought she was just being stupid and she hadn't guessed anyway, so there. I half turned and said Macdui would do, the hill we'd decided to climb this trip. A quiet descended but I knew I'd disappointed Judy who quickly resorted to her Nintendo. As usual Fiona was dozing and I could see her bare feet twitching beside me as I drove. We'd been going to the chalet for several years, even before the kids came, away from the rush of the city to revive ourselves in the quiet. Getting up with the birds, the light on the curtains and that warmth from the wooden floors was what I dreamed about at my paper-strewn desk when a thin Edinburgh drizzle coated my office window. Now we were there again, this time an October break with some walking before the snow came.

We tumbled from the car and looked around as we always did, as if we had been transported to some magical world whose meaning was new to us. When we went inside (the door always left daringly unlocked by Mrs Sneddon), there on the table would be a vase of honeysuckle and a plate with some shortbread. Too late for the flowers of course, but the shortbread was there. The comfort of certainties!

I was born in the city and it wasn't till I was in my thirties that work took me to the hills. My firm was involved in building the funicular up Cairngorm and I spent many days there with my boss supervising the project. I remember how hard a time we got sometimes in the local hotels and pubs for many saw what we were doing as a rape of the landscape. They thought we were taming the wilderness in some way. To me it was a job, but I believed at the time it would open up the hills to more people. I remember one old guy telling me that the Grey Man would get his revenge, before he staggered off. Bill and I laughed and that night trudging along the road back to our B and B with a mist coming in over the tops, Jim suddenly shouted 'Look man, it's the Grey Man!' I remember I hated him for making me jump.

Since then the hills have had a pull on me and from an early age the kids have been pulled that way too. Fiona loves books more than boots and maintains those are the only cliffhangers she's into. God bless her.

That summer there had been a programme about the Cairngorms on TV and James was keen to go up on the funicular. It was quite a distance to drive from the chalet so we booked an overnight in Aviemore. Fiona would amuse herself in the town while we would climb Cairngorm and then Macdui and take it from there. I was keen to show the kids my handiwork and point out a few landmarks.

It had been an indifferent summer but September had given us some sunshine so our hopes were high for a dry walk. Certainties indeed! The forecast had been for light showers from the West but as soon as the boot slammed shut a light rain began. We had plenty of rainwear with us and accompanied by some mutterings from Judy about wishing she'd gone with her mum, we set off. They liked the train and the changing landscape as it moved but I decided to go easy on trying to elicit anything approaching enthusiasm.

Fearlas Mor

On the top the cold hit us suddenly. We had to get going so I told James to take the lead while I'd take the rear. He was a young lad and that kind of responsibility thrilled him. There were a few people about but the time of year seemed to have kept numbers low. I was excited for the kids as we moved up and the valley stretched out behind us. We lingered for a bit at the top then headed towards the summit of Macdui. 'Second highest peak in Britain, James,' I boasted, and urged them on through the rubble of boulders and crisp packets and tissues. I thought of those predictions the moaning minnies had made years before but we passed older people who wouldn't have been here without the funicular. I could tell by their voices how amazed they were by the views. More amazed than my kids!

As we walked the rain became serious and drips appeared at the end of our noses. I had a brief vision of Fiona sitting in a cafe with a book drinking coffee but it quickly disappeared as my boot slipped on a boulder. A shaft of pain shot through my ankle and I feared the worst. I sat down, undid my laces and rubbed it vigorously. It was just grazed. The skin looked angry and it was damn painful but I knew I hadn't done any serious damage. Oddly in all those years it was the first time I'd ever hurt myself in the hills and I was angry. The kids were anxious as well as wet now, but I reassured them that I was fine and that the weather forecast was for brighter skies later. If we just kept going it would be worth it in the long run. James was getting peckish of course, his growing body craving food every hour. I told him we'd be on Macdui in no time and we'd find a place to shelter and eat. As I said this I knew what a lie it was, as I had a recollection of the bareness up there. Shelter was not easily come by in this terrain.

Since Cairngorm a thick mist had swept in and I took the lead across the plateau determined to keep to the path. After an age it seemed (my memory had told me it wouldn't take long) we eventually reached the summit cairn on Macdui. Although the rain had eased, there was no view, only the sweep of low dirty clouds that appeared in the breaks in the mist. I began to shiver. It had suddenly gone even colder. As we leaned against the cairn I turned to look at Judy and saw the firm set of her mouth. I felt for her, up here in this when she'd rather be down there in the warmth. I knew that she'd done it for me, braved this because she knew I wanted to point out familiar places and to show her the train. Normally she was pretty lively whatever the weather but today she was sullen and silent. She said she was cold and I said it would get warmer when we descended and offered her a swig from the flask of tea but she shook her head. James had gone round the hill a little and had disappeared. I thought he was probably having a pee. I hadn't thought of the danger at all. I rummaged in my rucksack for my map but I couldn't find it: insect spray, compass, harvest bars, swiss-army knife, an old sock, some green twine, but no map. Crazy. I'd never gone into the hills without a map. I could only imagine that some stupid complacency had made me careless. I'd been going on all the previous evening about how I knew every boulder up there! OK, there was one I didn't know! It wasn't the end of the world though, for I'd decided that we should probably count our losses and go down before the rain started again. Then I began to look round for James. He'd been gone for about five minutes or more and now I realised how foolish I'd been not to alert him to the danger of the crags in this visibility. I told Judy to stay there with my rucksack while I'd fetch him. She nodded and said she'd have a harvest bar.

As I made my way to the right a figure appeared through the mist. He was tall and his hood was up but I just caught a glimpse of his beard as he passed. I asked if he'd seen a young boy but he merely strode on past with the easy gait of a mountaineer. Thanks mate! I knew James had gone this way and he couldn't have gone far. By this time the mist was even denser and I was pushed to see ten feet in front of me. I thought about Judy waiting there but decided I had to find James. A growing anger made my hands shake. I'd felt this before when the kids had done something foolish and the repercussions affected as all. Selfish. It was so bloody selfish to go wandering away in this. I picked my way gingerly, aware of the pain in my ankle but walking didn't seem to be aggravating it. I shouted James's name and stood listening for a reply. Again, louder, I cupped my hands and bellowed " JAMES!" There was nothing. Now my anger was turning into concern. I could actually feel the transition as if something in my head had passed down into my chest. Now a chill slithered through me and made me shiver. I remember cursing. Damning and bastarding at no one, but it was an outlet for the churning inside. A vision of Fiona came to me then: my beautiful wife holding her coffee cup while one of her children was lost on a mountain. I felt my breath quicken. Judy! I must go back to Judy I thought, and then both of us will go round the other side and look for him. Perhaps he's already back at the cairn. I smiled at the thought. Why hadn't that occurred to me before now! He'd gone right round and was now back with Judy, worried about me. I saw the cairn, but further to the left than I'd remembered. I could see a figure: one figure. My chest began to drum and I brushed my wet cheeks. My hands were red and slippy and my wrists were sweating under the cuffs of my anorak.

She greeted me as if she'd given up the idea of ever seeing me again. 'Dad! I thought it was James but it was another person,' she gasped.

'Yes, I spoke to him.'

'Where's James, Dad?'

'I don't know sweetheart. He can't be far away.'

I hugged her and told her it would be fine. We held hands and made for the other side of the cairn. In a couple of seconds the rain started again, a thin drizzle that settled on our hair and faces and with it a wind. Suddenly we heard a cry. We looked at each other for a second then I pulled Judy with me towards its source. We skipped over rubble and brittle grass and then the cry came again, sharper. A raven! It was up there. Another. It wasn't James.

Judy fell over once and reassured me that she was OK. We slowed. I felt another twinge in my ankle then I remember seeing a shaft of pale light falling ahead, probably to the West but I couldn't be sure. The clouds were parting. My spirits lifted a notch. Things would be simpler if we could see where we were. I was sure we'd be able to see James if the mist blew off. He was probably squatting down somewhere waiting to be found.

I kept stopping and listening, then shouting. It was a way of trying to calm Judy, trying to make her believe that I was in control, that if I kept listening then moving purposefully she wouldn't guess how afraid I was. And I was. It was as if things were slipping away from me. My son was lost, however temporarily and I had allowed it to happen. I couldn't see anything and therefore I could be wandering round in circles. Was this girl going to rely on me for her safety? If only she knew how tenuous my control was. Then she said we should stop. Stop and wait. Sit and wait for the mist to clear because it seemed to be getting brighter. That's what she said and I wanted to believe her. I looked up and sure enough it was brightening. The mist was being blown over our heads by the gentle breeze and gradually hills were appearing on the right. I cuddled her and rubbed her shoulders and back and she did the same to me. I never loved this child more. I made some crack about Everest being a doddle after this and realised how stupid that was. But sure enough, a landscape was appearing as if painted, left to right, the sun like a blessing coming from the South West across The Devil's Point. Our spirits rose and we began to shout again hoping that

Fearlas Mor

the sound which had been strangled by the roiling mist, might travel. Then there was another sound. Ravens again? We both looked up and there they were soaring high to the West where the Lairig Ghru now appeared snaking far below. But the sound wasn't the ravens: it was longer and deeper than their cries. We looked at each other and scrambled towards it. I held her tight because we were now close to the steep crags leading down to the valley. And then we saw him: a small hudddled figure, his blue anorak vivid beside a huge boulder forty feet below us. I left Judy and carefully made my way down to James who had now seen me and was scrambling his way up. 'James! James! Stay there!' I cried. I couldn't stop shouting his name and he was shouting at me too. I'd rarely felt such exhilaration in my life as I reached him and clasped him to me but when I held him at arm's length and looked at him, there was something in his eyes which startled me - a terror which I wasn't expecting. He was shaking and when we pulled apart he was staring at the ground not at me. 'It's OK, you're safe now.' I said trying to reassure him, but he shook his head.

'No, no, he's still there," he gasped.'

'Who's there?'

'The man. He was chasing me. Dad he was after me. I couldn't get back to you.'

'What man? There's no-one else here James. Just take some deep breaths. You got lost, that's all. It's all over now.'

It was then I remembered the man I'd seen earlier: the sullen striding man who'd ignored my question. I decided not to pursue the matter but to get the hell back up and get my son back safely, so I led him slowly up through the mossy boulders and back to Judy.

The sun was stronger now and low, and as we neared the plateau James suddenly stopped and cried out 'Look it's him!' Across the valley on a misted ridge surrounded by what seemed a water-colour box of shades was a strange figure. I'd never seen a Brocken Spectre but I realised that must be what we were seeing. The low sun, the mist across there and our shadows. But there was only one figure there and that couldn't have been our shadows for we were close together. When reason fails to satisfy, you fall back on instinct. I waved my arms wildly hoping that the figure would do the same. It didn't. It had moved up the ridge now and changed shape. It seemed bigger with long legs, compassed as if to preserve its foothold. As I looked, I pulled James closer and told him it was our shadow and it often happened on mountains. Not to worry, it was just the sun and the mist. 'There's Judy up there, look.' As I said her name I heard a shriek from where I'd left her and she began scrambling down towards us. 'Dad! Dad!' she cried, 'I'm coming!'

The ravens had gone now but I could distinctly hear a new sound as a background to Judy's cries. My heart was pounding as I wrestled with the enigma of the Spectre and I suppose I was susceptible to any new anxiety, but this strange groaning sound seemed beyond comprehension. Judy reached us and for a moment we became one as if welded together by fear. The sound faded to be replaced by the clatter of stones. As if someone were scrambling down the ridge to our right. I realised in a moment of clarity that we had to retrace our steps up to the plateau and back to Cairngorm, that going down into the valley was madness: the weather might deteriorate again leaving us miles from our car and home.

'Now listen to me,' I said, trying to smile. 'There's nothing to be afraid of. We got separated but now we're together again and we're going back the way we came because mummy will be waiting for us. Now stick close and watch where you put your feet.'

James was about to speak but I stopped him with an emphatic 'Let's go!'

We climbed slowly and carefully back up and stopped briefly at the trig point where I assured them how quickly we'd covered the ground. The truth was I was petrified. I'd heard the groaning and I'd seen the spectre and that pub came back into my mind. The Grey Man. Oh very funny. A joke. A professor's tale to enliven a dull assembly. A tourist invention like Nessie… Stones again!

We crossed the plateau and the mist seemed to drop with us. Then I heard it again; the groaning sound. We hurried on and the ravens called overhead. 'Don't listen' I kept telling myself, 'just keep moving.' Judy was sobbing now, an inconsolable heaving that shook her whole body, and I could feel her hand turning hard as iron in my palm. James seemed to have calmed but he refused to take the lead and clung to my rucksack which jerked with each step.

We reached the funicular and sat close in silence. The sun had gone and even the lower altitude was not enough to warm us. We removed our gear and drove back to Aviemore where Fiona was waiting anxiously.

That night the kids slept with us in our room and the next morning we drove back to the chalet. We'd unpicked the day endlessly and I felt buffeted by Fiona's looks.

As we drove up the tarred road past the huge rhododendron bushes a man passed us. I caught a clear sight of his beard as he passed for he turned and smiled before striding on. Fiona turned to me and said 'That's Mr McDuff , the man who spoke to me in Aviemore in the bookshop. He told me about The Grey Man.'

LADS

The lads are out. In thrall to the rain and the rottenness. You'll see them scurry, their eyes twinkling in among the mash of things unwanted, unloved, untended. This is the town where the scurrying things find all they need. Keep the cats in, keep in the dogs, the children, if you love them. Send out the men with tattoos, with thick legs for kicking, with fingers toughened by scars and nicotine. Let them bring sticks for a beating. The stick is a wonderful thing for a beating. Lash and thump and the crashing on the skull, the back, the leg. The baseball bat is a fine thing, its heft like a weighted gift. It has learned only one word. It lives for the strike, the crunch, the splintering bone. Too good for a ball. Let the bat sing and in the swinging let right be done on the lads. Let lads feel our blows till the brains ooze.

They come from up the Avenue. Out when the night comes, the bush blackens, the street springs below the air-soles, the trackies shish, the lamp-posts spill their thin light. They wave no goodbyes, come and go as they choose: to eat, to pull themselves, to lie still under their half-yanked curtains.

Then more emerge. Two lads and then another two. Bred from who knows what dark fissure, they mass for the forage, the skirmish. Swig- swig, the Cider, the Monk's brew, pull on the ciggie, the drag, the smoke swirl in the lungs that enervates. The rain is nothing - water off a lad's back, this rain. Call this rain! Then the park where the little kiddies fear to go. A swing. The lads love a swing - creak, creak, up and up the trainers kick the trees, the Chipper's reek so rich, the swish of cars on the main road and they fly. The lads will fly tonight.

Big man, you are your chair and your chair is you. Its arms are yours, its seat knows your arse, bowled by it. It is your friend, your citadel. This is a safe chair.

The TV chatters its senselessness, flashes different worlds, strange voices, people you don't understand. The curtains are drawn against the dark for the dark has eyes. Wife back there moves, innocent in her world of plates and pans but you are waiting, alert, fag burning down in spite of her. They'll come. You know they'll come again tonight, the tormentors, the un-settlers, the spreaders of disease here where decent men only want to live in peace.

There on the mantel is Tommy's photo. Tommy the bowler, the family man, the father of good sons, ruined by lads. You weren't near that night but you can picture the light from his open door - the dim lamps humming and his wife shouting after him to come back to the warm, the light. He'd gone after them, the lads who'd struck once too often. They'd taunted his son Willie for his trouble, poor Willie that couldn't even cry so well off-beam he was, but would laugh as they spat their hate-words: Daftie… fuckin daftie… fuckin vegetable… scumcunt. Tommy had calmed him, stopped his laughter with a slap till the tears came with the blood. Then he'd waited till he heard them beating the cars as they went back up the Avenue. Maggie said to forget it and he'd looked at her, said, not the first time but the last time they'll do this and she shook her head not knowing what to say, the cure worse than the disease. And he left her, running, shouting. Tommy, your friend. Tommy the cripple now.

But the lads remember wrongs done them; feel the ache of rejection, the dishonour of words shouted. Their brains can't untangle the nexus of cause and effect, the sociologist's psycho- babble. Lads just want to eat us all, to spread what they spread, to gnaw into the fabric of peace, to rend it till it comes apart and only the shreds are left.

Shreds in the head: the tangles of hate and fear, the ganglions swelling, the gangrene's suppuration. They've been. You can sniff them. They aren't far away, inside us or out. Are you a lad, big man? Do you feel a slither somewhere deep? Is it eating you up, trying to get out? Did you ever see Alien? That thing that burst out? It's in all of us. Maybe only lads can kill their kind.

Big man picks up his paper turns to the back page, sees that striker who never strikes, thinks if I had half his chances… A thump of metal, laughter, mumbled words, more laughter shrill in the dark. They're here tonight, the lads. He switches off the light, moves to the curtain, uncovers a sliver of window. Only the streetlamp's eerie flicker on the bonnet of his Astra. Then a can clatters, a foot thrown out to kick it on. They cherish the sound of metal. The voices louder now, the volume cranked, the shrieks of the pack: subsumed, every human leaning, in the hunger for belonging. The shibboleth: what he says you do: what you say you only offer.

She's heard them and she's through, just as Maggie was, saying no, don't do it, leave them they'll wander off. She's of the gentle land of milky kindness, where hands know only work or love, where voices are soft and smiles are open doors. But no, he's in the hall the bat up and his fist tight round it, his blood up, surging, every muscle filling, adrenaline expanding her tattooed name. If they touch the car they're for it, I mean it Jean, this time I mean it, it can't go on - we've got a right to peace. Then there's a thud on metal near and then another as they trash the cars.

His heart's pumping, his legs like iron to carry him forward, arms stiff for retribution. Four cowled heads slinking, turning, spitting words like lobbed stones and he's at them in the dimness, his club still as he runs till they turn like rats do in a stripped rick with nowhere to run, rearing for a last bite.

Near them, he stops, a car by him smashed, the shards crunching under his shoes.

The fruits of their genius - the release of destruction: the ripped, the smashed, the torn, the gashed, the battered, the bruised, the abused. If you gave them the sun they'd stomp it dull, pull stars from the sky and douse their light in a rusty bucket. Were the clouds to fall they'd pull them apart, wipe their noses and arses and flush them away. This is destruction incarnate: genius with a head that does the 360. This has cornered him, this big man with the word on his arm, Jean. And where is the next page of the script? Where is the next line, the move downstage, the cue that will ease the impasse? The bat lifts, the other hand takes hold for the two hander. He's the knight, his sword up for the smite as they fan out around him, smirking. And only now does big man fear the threat that is fanning, like the tendrils ink smokes in water. He feels them grasp him, doesn't know where to turn for there's no running now but hold his ground.

They find him crumpled, bleeding, hands stomped, head stomped till it's a balloon, his eyes tight with swollen lids. Love, love, she says and cradles him like her sick son long ago. He whispers I'm OK, OK, there's nothing else to say that wouldn't frighten her, this woman who loves him so much now. Then he's away, the neighbours pulled from their quiz shows, their Strictly This and Strictly That, their places in the sun; a moment here to know what lads can do, standing mute as the ambulance wails its way along and up the Avenue.

Lad's scoff and preen: we fuckin did that bastard in, where's the problem man, nobody within a fuckin mile to see a thing. Relax. Cunt had it coming. The stars are out, the room is small, a Celtic poster on the opposite wall and Kylie Minogue bending over in hot-pants. The others have gone home to lick their wounds. His work: an arm bashed, a shoulder dislocated, a mouth without its teeth. The hoods are down the faces drawn, pale, too many hours beneath the daylit sheets, too many mags, too many fags. Your mother's gone or father's gone and sister's got a baby from that bastard up the flats. Lads slink home, warning no-one say a word, we were at my place all the time. The old man's OK for an alibi.

The days were coloured cream or green, soused in chemicals, sounding of wind and rain in the tiny ward. A joiner nursed a broken leg, that old man just fell, the age he's at they do it all the time, falling over their feet, forgotten where to put them is what he says. She comes in every day, the same blue coat, some chocs, the paper though he's read it through and through: it's a long day, a hospital day. She tells him what's been going on, the police around and that nice constable that Steven knew at school. How everyone's been kind, they can't believe how anyone could… Those lads, he says, they're hiding out in houses round about, with gardens just like ours, with fathers who pass our window, mothers who shop at Hussein's. Don't ask how anybody could - they did, they do, they will. She fidgets with her bag, goes back home to the kitchen, her plates and cups and fresh-baked scones while he lies, pillows stacked, nursing a secret child that sucks him dry of love.

A lad in the Pakistani's shop, hooded. No trouble here, his mother said he gave her credit when the old man lost the lot. Five hundred quid on Celtic for the cup, the telly on full blast, the dish vibrating with the tension of a bet. Then those two goals, the world came crashing down. Brave face the only face she knew; he'd talked her into it, and now she shared the shame of loss. Hussein had laughed, said he'd never understood this football thing - the green, the blue - he was a cricket man. Lad laughed, said I like bats but not that kind, and Hussein laughed too.

Big Man's home at last, the steep stairs agony. Bone rages against bone and in the skull things happen that he doesn't understand. He can't keep still, drops dishes on the floor, sees the tremor of his knife at table. Sometimes he sits, no TV on and starts to cry, knowing no reason. The days begin to lengthen. Spring bulbs burst out in yellows, reds and blues and he totters to his shed to sit and watch the birds. But lads keep crawling back into his brain, sleek smirking things that come and come. They're on his tongue, she shakes her head and tells him stop, it isn't any use going on and on. He nods, says yes, he's sorry just you close your ears, it's just I can't forget as easily as you.

Six weeks he'd been back home, and in his shop Hussein hears more, of bats and striking, and he'd had enough. He told a copper all the lad had said and things moved on. The lads were trapped, bared teeth, but lost. They caged them for a month or two.

He hears it on the news, goes to his shed and thinks of a belt around his neck. He knows the hook would never hold. Besides, the nights are quieter now, peace settling gently like unexpected snow.

PINK WELLIES

I've been home with my father for three days now. He wouldn't go to mum's funeral but I needed to see him, needed to get closer to her, to be here. Inside, the house feels becalmed, like the ship in that poem. I suppose anywhere would feel quiet compared to the constant throb at my Hall of Residence.

Now I hear him snoring two rooms away. At least it breaks the quiet. Long ago, silence killed this house; scooped it hollow as if it were an orange. Though my folk were never chatty, there was a warm quiet between them then, with just my voice breaking it, for anything I said or did seemed to enrage him. Now his quiet is cold: a grey quiet the colour of those curtains.

His snoring has stopped. Now it's the pad of his feet to the toilet. I'll pillow my ears. I hate the dribble of his pee, his fart, so intimate, so uninhibited as if it's a trumpet call saying 'I am up, ready to take on the day.' He chaps on my door, his low growl like Bob's when he's angry. 'Heather. Are you up.' Not a question, the intonation's wrong. A question would open the possibility of disappointment. A command. No answer needed. 'Heather' doesn't fit his lips. It's too soft somehow. He should have called me Agnes. One of the old, hard names. He could gnash on the 'G.' It'll be the only time he'll say my name today. Since I've come back, I'm just a body, something familiar that fills a space; the one who'll do for him: his kitchie deem, for God's sake. He never looks in my eyes. His eyes are always out the window on the sky. For the next few days, I'll have to rehearse my name to remind myself I exist. It's a coat I wear for others, my name, not for him. Deep in the cave of his skull, I must exist, though God knows in what form. Enough. I see the clock now. Twenty past seven. Damn. And I said I'd get his breakfast.

He's gone. The half-eaten porridge left by the sink. I can imagine him cursing me as he splashes down the track. Said she'd be up, make my breakfast. He's a kind of underkeeper now at the estate the other side of Arford. When mum left, he curled around himself like burning paper, turned his face to the wall, a resentment that took him, made him hate everything and everyone. He'd lost his job at the Massie's farm before that and moped about day after day, the glass in his hand mid-morning, his temper a fuse lit by the spark of every innocent word. Their customary silence became as brittle as crystal and shattered time and time again, those days. Then he heard that Lady Reid's keeper wanted help and his pal Zander said he'd put a word in. Well, he'd been a cowman all his days but he said he'd give it a go. Last night I pumped him a little about it and he said he misses the cows and the place for a grouse is in a bottle, but he's still at it.

He's been on his own now for two years. That black frying pan's his best friend: the stink of sausages and eggs always there in this same kitchen where I'd puddle in flour while mum baked scones or sometimes made those chocolate cakes that he loved. I stand now, the thin drizzle shutting out the distant hills. I can just make out the old Massie farmhouse like a big pearl in the mirk. It seems to have grown. I remember the gossip at the time they let him go: that the Massie's Angus bull had tried to loup a ditch and broken a leg; that their eldest, Lewis had been found with cannabis at the Academy; that Annie Massie was thin as a rake with cancer. Everything was falling apart there, they said, with that grin the old ones kept for others' misfortune. Then suddenly they were selling up, the farm to be sold park by park, that fine rolling land that had been a part of my childhood, turned into a History Theme Park. On clear days, you could hear whoops and cries like demented birds as the helmeted Romans re-enacted skirmishes with the painted locals. I've never been myself but on the way to school, we'd pass buses rolling up from all over, bursting with school kids clutching their worksheets.

The land round here has changed so quickly. Farms I knew as a kid just melt away: the Baikie's turned into a restaurant; the Wilson's, the Thain's, both bought and gentrified, grey farm houses and tumbling byres bought and done up, their yards paved in red bricks to support the four-by-fours that drive East each day to sip from the black gold.

At the time mum first said she was going, I sat my Highers. Bent low over my English booklet, half-full of her tears, half-full of Willy Loman's shattered dreams, I scribbled furiously and by some miracle, I passed them all. He seemed proud, though he never said so. But a pair of pink wellies from Stranoch's Store appeared by my bed a few days after. I thanked him and he nodded, said they'd do for the puddles if the poor summer kept up. Pink wellies. Me? Mum should have known better, but perhaps he did it on his own. She'd taken a job in a Newsagent's in Arford after he was sacked - a cramped cluttered shop that tried to meet every need from fishing permits to tights, but she loved it and one night she told me she had 'feelings' for the man who owned it, a tall, balding man who rarely smiled. She'd been knitting and she let it rest in her lap and looked at me. I remember staring at a log that was quivering with heat while her words edged out like a difficult calving. I cried and clattered upstairs for I knew it was the end for us all. I knew she loved me and yet she'd let some stranger into our house. After that, I tried to keep out of her way. I felt she'd betrayed us, though I knew she wasn't happy with him. Then one afternoon I came back from ferreting and she'd gone. No note that I ever saw.

For a few nights I heard him sobbing in the dark but by day he went on as if nothing had happened, gruff as ever. I wanted to hug him so much then but I couldn't do it, afraid that something held tight in him would burst and he'd hate me for it. It seemed so deep and dark that I was afraid to see it I suppose. Someone said they'd seen him parked outside the shop just sitting there but it had changed hands by then and mum had gone to Perth.

It was soon after she left that I met the new owners of the Massie place. He spoke to me one day when I was out with Bob on The Sandy Sheugh, asking who I was and why wasn't I at school. Cheeky bugger, I thought, but I was polite. Told him I was taking a year out to decide what I wanted to do. He laughed and said he'd a good deed for me if I felt like it. Evidently his wife, Deirdre was a bit depressed and he thought some female company would help. I remember the way he flicked his blond hair out of his eyes. I said I'd think about it. Deirdre. I had a wee chuckle over that. Kept saying it aloud, in as many posh voices as I could muster. It was a name you found in novels but you never expected to meet someone called that. Well, not round here.

I'd been to the Massie's before of course, at Hogmanay and once for a party, but that day as I walked up the hill, all I saw seemed strange. A black sign on the dyke said 'An Taigh Geal' in gold letters. I knew it must be Gaelic. The pot-holed track had been tarred, the old garden had been fenced behind a big iron gate and round the house, the drive was soft with a golden gravel that crished under your feet. There was a blue alarm of some sort above the door. What with the fence and everything, it was more like a fortress than a house. They'd ripped up the old lawn and the flower beds and chopped down the yew by the front door. The walls had been whitewashed and a new door with glass panels caught the low sun. When the door opened, a dark-haired woman in jeans and suede boots and a floppy cardigan greeted me. Inside the wooden floors gleamed in the light from the wide windows. It seemed as if a whole wall had been made of glass and the room looked huge. Leather settees surrounded a stove with a shiny flue, and there was a smell of wood and leather and the sweet smell of baby which I recognised from my Aunt's house. This was Deirdre of course, pretty and chatty, not the glum depressed woman I was expecting. I gave her the little posy of flowers I'd picked as a handsel and her eyes lit up. Then a baby cried upstairs and I remember being shocked when she said she was mother to "that" as if it were a nuisance or something. She went up and brought it down and put the sweet little thing into a frilly cot and asked if I'd like some tea. 'You probably take milk and sugar do you?' she said, and I said I did. We chatted about country life. She was from London. She'd met Malcolm at University in Aberdeen. He was an engineer in the oil industry, something to do with mud, she said, laughing, and then she said it was true, there was money in muck. I'd never heard the saying. If you'd said that to me, then I'd have thought you meant cows or something. God knows there's no money in them. We talked for a while and I told her about school and exams and Dad being a keeper. She asked about mum and I told her she'd gone and she smiled as if she already knew. She kept touching me, on the arm, on my hand, leaning towards me and staring at me as we spoke. Her breath smelled of peppermint. I felt as if I were with someone from another world whose habits were strange, but I liked her, for she made me feel that she was listening to everything I said. When I left, the sun had gone down and on the walk back I couldn't get the smells and sights of the place out of my head.

Ours was once a tied cottage, but he bought it from the Massie's years before. Mum used to pester him about the carpet and the fireplace and how old and tatty they were, but nothing happened. That day it seemed to me that we lived in a time-warp: welcome to the Fifties farm cottage folks - beige tiles round a beige fireplace, chipped and scalded by burning logs; a patterned carpet whose colours have long since faded, its weave unravelling to trip the unwary foot. Where they have the scents of pine, we have Bob's dubious scents and his hairs. He was getting old even then and the smell of wet lab had seeped into the walls. The sink in the bathroom upstairs was white enamel with hair cracks that fooled your nail to lift them, the taps always dripping, the stairs with their own creaking music. And I was used to it. Until that day I met Deirdre and realised what the Twenty-first Century meant.

I saw a lot of her after that, and although there were years between us in age and experience, she became like an older sister to me, the secrets we shared. She didn't seem to go out much or see many people but she made me laugh when she tried to mimic the Doric. I remember trying to teach her to say 'Foo's yir aal maan?' which she managed in her own way. My reply would always be 'He hisna his sorras tae sik,' a phrase that had stuck to Mr Massie once like a sticky willy. We'd fall about laughing and I'd cuddle wee Jamie and we'd drink tea without milk or sugar and she'd tell me about how Malcolm loved the country.

One day though she seemed distant, almost as if she didn't want to speak at all and the next time I called her voice seemed odd and she said she had to go out. That was the last time I saw her before I heard that she was in Cornhill Hospital in Aberdeen. It was Malcolm told me she'd taken pills and he'd been terrified that he'd got home too late. She never came back to the house after that and he'd sold up and bought a house in Aberdeen where his mother looked after little Jamie. There's new folk in now, but I haven't met them for I left for Uni soon after Deirdre went. I got a Christmas card from her that year with a

London postmark with the simple words 'Foos yir awl man? Love, Deirdre.' I didn't show it to him of course; he'd always called them 'Oilies' which I hated, but I took it with me back to Uni in the January where I'd take it out and think of her, that lovely girl who couldn't cope with life.

Now I'm back walking in the rain with Bob trailing behind me. I won't go far, for I know the struggle it is for him now. Perhaps the pink of my wellies will help him see me. My finals are this year and I've brought my books with me, though God knows how I'll concentrate with so many memories crowding in. It'll be mince for his tea tonight. I know how much he likes mince. Perhaps it'll make him smile. Perhaps.

CARAMEL WAFERS

One night the bear suddenly burst into a verse of 'You are my Sunshine.' By chance, she'd pressed the little red padded heart on his paw and it happened. He did seem to miss out a couple of words in the middle of the song but she didn't mind that. He's company, she told herself, and it stopped her talking to slices of bread, a habit that had alarmed her sons in the past.

A couple of weeks before, she fell getting off a bus. As she lay there, she bled milk from the carton which had burst in her bag. It was all over the pavement. The driver was kind and left his cab and helped her to her feet to rest on the narrow bus-stop bench.

'What a mess I've made,' was all she could say, but a nice woman in a pale coat told her not to worry, they'd get her an ambulance just to be on the safe side. They took her to Casualty at the Vic then kept her in to do "tests" they said.

Her daughter Denise appeared out of the blue one day bringing her a cardboard box with six tins of Baxter's soup, two tins of processed peas (which she hated) and a tin of ham. She had a needle in her wrist attached to a drip and her thin arm was black and blue as if she'd been mauled by a wrestler. She didn't care. She thanked her for the tins, though inside she thought it was a daft present to take someone in hospital. She'd had a nice card from Bob, she said, huge, with roses you could feel.

'Sorry you had a wee fall mum. I'm coming to see you on the fifteenth. Get some caramel wafers in.

Love Bob.'

'Well, you'd notice it anyway,' Denise said, putting it back on the locker. She hoped Malcolm, who worked abroad wouldn't worry too much. Mother seemed fine.

A couple of days later an ambulance took her home. She returned with special padded knickers which felt like armour, and a new zimmer with wheels this time. Hip bones were very fragile they'd said, she'd need to take care. "Fragile" was her middle name these days, it seemed. Apart from the jelly legs and the aches that seemed to wander round her body, she found her hands had begun to shake a bit when she was trying to pull on her tights, a task that seemed to take most of the morning now. 'Where does the time go?' she'd say, when anyone would listen. Now as she stared at the blue flowers on the carpet, she remembered Bob was coming to see her. He'd phoned the night before to remind her. He'd said something about a conference. He didn't come very often, but she knew how busy he was. She lifted the little bear and kissed him. Every night before bed, she did this and sang along to his song, but last night, for some reason, he wouldn't sing. She thought Bob might be able to fix him and then he'd hear his song.

Bob had said he'd be there about two and it was either twenty-past, or fifteen- minutes-to, or six-thirty by the three clocks in the room. Time stood still for Agnes, for she hadn't the fingers to fiddle with batteries anymore. It seemed everything around her had either stopped working or fallen or broken. Just that morning her pine toilet-roll holder had clattered from the wall as she pulled some tissue and the woman who came to clean said the Hoover wasn't picking up. Just keeping up was such a struggle. 'Never thought I'd ever be as hopeless as this,' she said to herself. None of these little calamities would have taken more than a few seconds to fix, but she was beyond that. Just as she'd got used to the daily ritual of taking her fifteen pills of various shapes and colours that she kept in a plastic bag, the warden appeared with a dispenser: a big

Caramel Wafers

plastic tower of a thing with seven storeys and wee compartments in each. You had to pull out Monday and put your pills in the morning, lunchtime, evening and night compartments. What a carry-on it all was.

'This will be easier,' Mrs Forsyth the warden had said, 'You'll know exactly which ones to take and when.' Why was it that everything which was supposed to be easier ended up being more difficult?

The doorbell buzzed and because the television wasn't on she heard it clearly. She made her slow way to the intercom in the hall and asked who it was.

'It's me mum, Bob,' came a deep voice from outside.

'Oh, I should've known it would be you. In you come, son.' She opened the door of the flat and saw the tall figure of her son closing the outside door. He strode towards her and smiled. He had a lovely smile. Even as a baby. He opened his arms with a big gesture and enveloped her like a bear. She felt a kiss on the top of her head. No-one kissed her lips anymore she noticed. He was warm and smelled like flowers. As they pulled apart and he stood looking at her, she felt like a girl again, shy.

'You look ravishing, mother dear!' he said, smiling again.

'Oh, thanks son, I'm fine. Come away in. You're looking well. Would you like a cup of tea or a drink? I've got some lager left over from Christmas.'

'Which Christmas would that be then? Tea will be fine mum. I'll make it if you like. You go and sit down.' She liked it when he made himself at home.

He felt the weight of the kettle, switched it on. He took one of the two tea bags left in the old caddy, shook off some tea-dust and looked into the street. On the opposite side was a large "Budget Garage" sign and mechanics in blue overalls buzzing about in various repair bays. A blonde woman clasping a little dog was stepping into a silver four-by-four and somehow it reminded him of London. He fingered the dusty plastic daffodils in a vase on the sill and shuddered at his mother's taste.

Tea took longer than he'd planned for the kettle wouldn't boil. Then he remembered his mother always pulled the plug from the socket. She lived in constant fear of electricity, bills, unlocked doors and running out of toilet paper. Every plug in the house when not in use was removed from its socket.

'You're looking well, mum' he said, sipping his dreadful tea. He'd become an Earl Grey man and this tasted like tar. The flat was unbearably hot and he felt the skin on his face prickle.

'Things OK then?' Bob felt mild panic that conversation might dry up, but he thought he'd use objects in the room to keep it going. As she replied, mumbling something about her legs and how hopeless her carers were, his eyes roamed. Photos of Denise and her family, of him and his, in the silver-gilt frame he sent last Christmas; the Edinburgh Crystal glasses that sat unused in the cabinet and the little tables of varying heights that occupied every available space. It always seemed remarkable to him how his father and mother felt so threatened by space. When you entered their living room you had to negotiate an obstacle course of chairs and sofas, occasional tables, pouffes and plastic covered boxes filled with knitting or newspapers. The move to here hadn't eased the congestion a bit, and now there was the zimmer.

'You've still got quite a lot of stuff in here mother,' he said, noticing the brown staining on the inside of his cup.

'I know Son, but I need it all. I lost lots of stuff when I moved.' She then lapsed into a catalogue of cookery books, specific garments and so on that she suspected her neighbour of plundering.

'But I've got wee Chucky there to keep me company.'
Bob turned to see the bear for the first time.

Caramel Wafers

'He won't sing anymore, Malcolm…er…Bob. Can you have a look at him? It might just be the batteries. I can't get him to work.'

'Bob. I'm Bob.' He smiled, irritated. It was one of her most annoying habits, the way she'd call him Malcolm then quickly correct it to Bob, but eager for any distraction, he picked up the bear, turned him round and undid the Velcro slit containing the battery box.

'Have you put new ones in?' He took them out with his expensive little silver penknife and placed new ones from the kitchen in the compartment. The phone went. He laid| the bear down beside him on the sofa.

'I think it might be for me, mum.' She thought it might be her daughter-in-law calling but when he put the receiver down a minute later he looked at her in a funny way and said he hoped she didn't mind but a woman who was also going to his conference and was a friend of his, was staying nearby and he wondered if she might come over.

'No, that'll be fine, son,' she said, a little taken aback. 'I'll away to the toilet.'

Bob pushed combed his fingers through his hair and looked at the bear. He shook his head at her silliness. A warm flutter of excitement stirred in him, the need to fix it superseded by the thought of seeing Emily. He crossed to the display cabinet, saw his broken reflection in the light from the window and ran his fingers through his hair again. There was a buzz from the outside door.

'I'll get that mum, it'll be Emily.'

Agnes sat and felt a little cheated that her time alone with him had to be shared. As she unspooled the toilet paper from the shelf, she could hear a woman's tinkling laugh.

Emily had taken off her sheepskin coat and placed it over a chair.

'This is Emily, mum. Emily this is my mother, Jean. Em's staying at the Holiday Inn up the road. We work in the same office actually, so it's nice that she can meet you at last.'

'I've heard a lot about you from Bob, Jean. This is a lovely little flat.' She wasn't sure she liked being called Jean by someone she'd just met and who was so young. The girl was sitting on the sofa with Bob now and she noticed that she was wearing fishnet tights. She was a bonny girl, right enough, much younger than her son who was now in his early fifties. There was something not quite right about them though. She noticed they kept looking at each other when they didn't need to. And they were sitting very close together.

'Nice and warm in here,' says Emily. 'My first visit to Scotland. I thought it might be rather cold but it's not too bad is it?'

'It's nice to meet you hen,' said Jean and Bob wondered why his mother had used that word: one he hadn't heard her utter in years. He hoped Emily wouldn't tease him about it later.

'I'm sure you'd like a wee cup of tea and a biscuit,' Jean said, and tried to raise herself from her chair, a process that involved bending double then tipping forward as the physio had shown her. Bob said not to bother, he'd get it.

'No, not at all, it's my house. I can do it fine,' insisted Jean, now upright, and determined. As she stood waiting for the kettle to boil, she thought the living room had gone very quiet.

'They'll be discussing the conference' she told herself, but underneath this thought, pushing it to the limits of credibility, was another more sinister one: Bob had always been a bit of a ladies' man and Jean had really liked his first wife Kitty. When he split from his second wife, Jean wondered if he was capable of being faithful. Now he has a girlfriend, Tanya, that Jean has never met. And now there's Emily.

Caramel Wafers

They were still sitting together, knees almost touching on the sofa when Agnes returned pushing the wheeled trolley. Whatever her name was, had taken on a bit more colour, Jean thought, offering her a cup and she's too smiley, as if she was up to something.

'Not too hot are you?" Jean asked the girl.

'No, no, I'm fine' said Emily, looking up and smiling. She stole a glance at Bob.

'How about my caramel wafers then, mum?' chirped Bob. 'Forgot about them didn't you.'

Agnes felt again that something had been stolen from her and Bob's cheeky tone grated.

'Haven't any. Sorry, son. Forgot all about them.' A wee goal had been scored.

'Not coming back here, then,' said Bob, nudging Emily gently. She laughed nervously. Between the women things unseen were passing that Bob would never understand. The way Jean sat, the tone of her voice, the lack of eye contact and the failure to provide the wafers, all combined to make the girl anxious to leave as soon as possible.

Emily asked about Dennis and his family and the weather "up here" as if, it seemed to Jean, this was the Arctic Circle or something. Why did they always seem surprised that you got Channel 4 or that you could get Earl Grey tea here? Not that she liked it anyway. It was as if the world revolved round London and nothing anywhere else was worth bothering about.

By this time Bob had become quiet, leaving all the talking to Emily. When Jean enquired about her grandson and her daughter-in-law Bob said they were fine but he didn't take out any photos as he usually did. He suddenly got up and asked if he could use his mobile phone. 'Just use my phone' said Jean, but he said it was business and he'd speak in the hall.

A few minutes later he returned and stood with his hands open, apologetically. 'Look mum, this is really bad timing, but something's cropped up at the conference and

I'm going to have to go and sort it out. These people never leave you in peace. I'm afraid I'm going to need some support from the office' he said, looking at Emily. She shrugged in a "what can you do?" way and put on her coat.

Jean felt that pain in her hip. She called it her "sad pain." Then she felt that warmth in her chest, which came mostly at night when she thought of her husband Tom. She watched Bob struggle into his coat. He smiled weakly at her.

They left with cheek kisses and hugs that were too tight. She could smell the girl's sweet perfume on her as she watched them walk down the path to the street. They bumped each other and laughed on their way to the gate. Jean was sure they were whispering to each other.

Jean knew the pain of partings, but this one hurt. What hurt more was the thought that she wouldn't see him again for a long time.

'He's my wee boy' she told herself as if she needed reminding. She wished she'd given him his favourite wafers now, but it was too late.

'I'm so stupid,' she thought, 'Just a stupid old woman.'

She waved them off at the window and stood staring long after they'd disappeared. She turned to look at the sofa for Chucky but he wasn't there; he was lying face down on the floor at one side as if he's been thrown there, the wires and battery box like spilled innards. She went down on her knees, every bone creaking and picked him up. The carpet stung. When she clutched his paw, the tune played again. She laughed. She lay down, drew her knees up and cradled him to her.

'You are my wee boy, my only wee boy…' she sang, and the new words fitted perfectly.

HERE'S TO SUCCULENCE

Now it was harder. They'd gone through the speed-dating stuff. Twenty quid for four minutes each of inane chat in a pub with stained tartan carpets and a couple of palm trees. She'd learned nothing about him. Why not just sit there and look at each other? That would be enough wouldn't it? He could wonder where she got that big scar over her lip and she could muse over the possibility that a nose that big might possess supernatural olfactory powers. It was Musical Chairs without the music, but by some minor miracle they were about to meet again. As she waited for him in Chez Pierre under the gaze of an interested waiter, her alter ego conjured a more up-front encounter…

'You don't have any STI's do you?' she'd say leaning back.

'Oh, well I've had syphillis of course,' he'll say, ' Practically runs in the family with us. But no-one's gone mad yet. Fucking painful needles though. Ever had it yourself?'

'No. Convent wouldn't let me out, nights. During the day, it was mostly prayers and digging spuds in the garden. Very self-gratifying.'

'Oh, right. Got you.' He'll move in his seat, uncomfortably, then he'll probably feel obliged to add, 'The old falling in the cucumber patch bit.' Before getting to the nitty with 'You're no oil painting are you? I mean, you're not exactly beautiful.'

Then she'll go for the jugular with… 'No. But let's face it, you're here because you can't get a shag. So someone like me is probably a good bet. Am I correct?'

'Well, I must say, for a nun you're pretty up-front and personal.'

'You really think I'm a nun?' she'll rage, and this is what she really wants: ' If I was a nun I wouldn't be sitting here with you, twat.' Of course she'd never been a nun, but he'd probably swallow it and the lie would feel as delicious as a chocolate éclair. Nor, it has to be said, would he have had syphilis. Too heavy. Perhaps a little touch of genital warts once after an injudicious interlude with an intoxicated holiday rep in Ibiza, but he's not going to come clean about that is he?...

Well, they'd ticked each other's "speeding tickets" together with the Italian waiter and the Swedish au pair, both of whom, it transpired, had made everybody's lists. So why did they come at all if they're so bloody attractive? She didn't really fancy the waiter much: when he looked at her she swore she could feel hands running up her legs. And he bit his nails. After about a dozen "dates" she was struggling to put anyone on her ticket, so she put him down together with Eric, the wee bald guy with the stutter from Cumbernauld, who was into Dusty Springfield. No, she didn't even ask. She thought she'd pop him down and then as an afterthought she put Sam, because she thought he looked vulnerable. Sam put her third, he admitted, though he was certain he'd seen his second, the P.A. from Rutherglen, on the "Chix Up for It" site, and the Swedish one didn't even make eye contact.

No, it's not like that. It's what do you do/ what interests do you have/ have you done this before, stuff. At the end of four minutes, each bloke moves on and all that's left is the sight of a fat backside, a fading vision of each face, and a craving for another rum and coke. Perhaps you remember how much hair the mechanic had, and wonder about cheap repairs to your creaking Fiat Panda. If you're a bloke, you might wonder at the pertness of Miss Sweden's tits, fighting for release from the Franz Ferdinand T-shirt.

Here's to Succulence

He's late. Maybe it's the rain. It's bucketing. Then he slopes in, slightly cowed.

'Shitty night. Sorry I'm late, er…Brenda,' he says. She smiles. She's not getting up for the kiss each cheek business. He's missed that. He sits. There are damp patches on his shoulders, and his hair is flat, as if he's been carrying a bag of tatties on it.

'Why didn't you wear a jacket?' she asks, 'The forecast was really bad.' They'd established an acceptable vernacular quotient after two minutes of their "chat" when she'd complained of the "fucking draft" in the pub and he'd thought she meant the beer.

'I gave it to Derek, my brother. I never wear a jacket in summer. I'm not averse to a bit of good old Glesga rain. Always fucking raining.' "Averse!" pulls her up. She hadn't imagined his vocabulary to be quite so extensive. 'And anyway, I like this shirt.' He pats the front as if it were an obedient dog, and picks up the huge menu. The shirt has broad stripes the colour of three-day-old vomit outside The Light of Krishnapur..

'Nice shirt,' she offers.

'Thanks. Not everyone likes it. Not a bad place is it? Derek's in the police and he knows the owner Pierre.' She feels a crack coming on about filthy kitchens and bribes but resists it. Cynicism can be exhausting. She's going to play this straight from now on. She looks at him over the menu and thinks he's got nice eyes. That's a start. The nose is quite big though.

'Are you having a starter?' he asks.

'No. I'll just have a main and see how it goes. Trying to lose a bit, actually.'

'You seem fine to me. Every woman I know seems to be on a diet for some reason.'

'Body image.'

'Haggis balls.' He wasn't really listening. Wondering whether to have a starter and keep her waiting or just to go for a main. The wee soul's trying to multi-task, she thinks: read a menu and have a conversation. Taxing.

'How women feel about their bodies.' The moment the words were out she knew they were a mistake. "Feel" and "bodies" – meaty bones to the sexist dog. He looked up and smiled.

'Gok Wan. He seems to know about women alright. But he's…you know…'

He hasn't smelled the bones or else has the sense to leave them lying. He watches Gok Wan?

'I can't watch that stuff without wanting to puke, 'she says, 'All those daft women who look about two hundred when they're only twenty-five. What's the point of giving some old witch of seventy, five thousand quid's worth of gleaming white gnashers and a new hair-do just to make her look sixty-five? You just know that when these programmes are over and the fifteen minutes of fame has gone, they'll rip off the glad-rags, kick off the heels and yank up the jeans to revert to however damned unhappy and ugly they were in the first place, gnashers or no gnashers.'

'Well. That's quite a speech. I'm sure you're right though.' And you're quite clever, Sam, to think I'm right, she thinks.

The waiter hovers, obviously relieved that the lady has a date and isn't one of those saddoes who eat alone, desperately engrossed her phone or a Tesco receipt to avoid any unwanted male eyes.

'Well, I think we're ready to order. OK?'

He orders the steak frites. She's having sea bass and salad. They've chosen a Pinot Noir at twenty quid. She wasn't sure, but he told her not to worry about the price. Will he pay for the wine? The menus gone, they're forced to look at one another. He lowers his eyes and laughs.

'What did you think of the other night: the dating, I mean?'

'Oh God. First time I'd done it. I was really nervous.'

Here's to Succulence

'I noticed you when they were giving out drinks. I liked your hair. The scrunchy thing.'

'Thanks. By the way, have you ever had syphilis?' Shit. Tongue why do you do this!

'What?' Keep it going, it might lead somewhere interesting, she thinks. She's happier in fantasy land anyway.

'Syphilis. Have you ever had syphilis?' The waiter arrives with the wine and after a convincing "pop" pours some into Sam's glass. Sam drinks and nods.

'No. Have you?'

'No. Wouldn't let me out of the convent.' He looks at her and leans forward.

'Are you a Roman Catholic then?'

'No. I think I'm a Jehovah's Witness really. You know those folk who come to your door and ask if you agree that the world's going to pot.'

'And you're one of them,' he says, scratching his nose.

'No.' The main courses arrive. The wooden phallus is ground with a professional flourish and they begin to eat.

'I'm getting a bit confused here,' he says. 'You were in a convent but you're not a Catholic but you think you're a Jehovah's Witness but you're not really.'

'I haven't joined up in the Kingdom Hall that's all, though I do think the world's going to pot. Don't you?'

'You're doing it aren't you?'

'What?'

'Knocking at my door. Trying to convert me.' He fills up her glass. 'How's the fish?'

'It's very good. Nice and succulent.'

'Succulent. You know my mother wouldn't let me say that word. She wouldn't let me say "knickers" either. She thought they were disgusting. Daft, isn't it.'

'Has it affected you adversely?'

'Yes, I think it has,' he says, 'It's made me a bit iconoclastic with language. Kicking back, I suppose. I try to say both as often as possible now that she's gone.'

'My, my. I don't think I've ever met a linguistic iconoclast before. You hide it well though.' She put down her knife and fork and drank some wine. He did the same. He looked at her and noticed that her scar was hardly discernible in the dim light. A strand of hair had fallen over her left eye. For the first time, he realised she was beautiful and the revelation chilled him. It was as if something superficial, amusing, diverting, had suddenly assumed a darker, more enduring feel. He felt himself climbing a ladder of silly words that each had erected against the other's fortress. Here he was up near the top and she was still climbing. Down there, below somewhere was where he lived. Up here the air was thin but sweet.

'Penny for them,' she said. She was discomfited by his silence and by the way he gazed at her. For the first time, she felt that words were failing her. She'd even used up her little fantasy routine and it had fallen short like an arrow fired from too far. Normally she wouldn't care: reload, shoot again with a different trajectory. But she began to feel that the words she threw at him were blowing back at her, soft fluttery words like snowflakes dropping from his lovely voice, melting on her as if they had turned to nothing. She wanted to hear him say her name. She wanted this game to stop being a game and for him to become real.

'Just enjoying the moment,' he said.

'That's good.' She began to eat again.

'Succulent. A very succulent steak, this, Brenda.' She looked up and lifted her glass to him.

'Here's to succulence in all its forms,' she said, smiling.

'I'll drink to that. And here's to Brenda in all her forms.'

She felt a warmth surge through her each time he said her name. She'd never felt that with anyone else. It was as if in saying her name he was giving her something. Silly. She'd come here armoured with all the cynicism she could muster. Invulnerable. Not really caring what damage she did. She always left them damaged in some way, could tell by the looks on their faces which would gradually darken as they realised she was impregnable. One of those women who wants and doesn't want; who's afraid to lay down her arms and sue for peace. Sometimes she wondered if they all knew how unhappy she was. How it wasn't they who were rejected, it was she who was rejecting herself.

'Brenda.'

'What?'

'You were miles away there.

'Sorry. Sorry Sam. It's not you. I was just thinking about something, that's all. I'm having a great time.'

The waiter brought the sweet menus. After a moment each looked up, pointing at the description of the pears in red wine…

'Succulent,' they said, in unison.

THE PARK

We're at the park with mum. I want to show her how high I can go on the swings. Kick and kick and up and up I go and the trees are rushing under my new trainers. If I go higher, I can kick the sky which is grey. My legs look funny as if they're just stuck onto my body when I kick them out, like my sister Kathleen's drawing of my mum. On the next swing, there's a girl with blonde hair who's trying to get as high as me, but I'm always up before her. I've never spoken to her but I know she's often here with her mum. After a time, I want to go down again but it always takes longer than you want. You tug one chain and you wobble a bit and it slows you. Sometimes I'll shout to mum and she'll try to stop me, but she grabbed the chain once and I fell off and grazed my knee. She says I should just be patient and stop by myself.

There aren't many kids here today. It's not raining yet but mum said it would rain later so we should go to the park early. My best friend Charlie has gone to see his gran in Scarborough but maybe Eric my second best friend will come soon and we can explore in the bushes. We made a hut there last time with some sticks we found and nobody could see us. It was great to be in there and watch people passing on the path. They didn't know we were there but a little dog found us and Eric put up his finger and told it to be quiet. It just looked at him and then dashed back out. I think we scared it. Mum's talking to that tall woman with the funny boots. She likes her. She says she's a kindled spirit but I don't know what she means. I suppose she likes her boots or something. They seem to be looking at the seats by the sandpit. There are some little ones in there throwing sand about. There'll be tears before bedtime, that's what mum says when you start having a good time. I'm going on the chute which is always sticky and spoils the slide. Some kids try to run up it and mum says that's why it loses its shine. I climb up but it's not very high. When I try to push myself off I don't move. You feel stupid just stuck there and then you have to push yourself down bit by bit while other kids are behind you shouting at you to get off. Mum's gone over to the seats and is standing near the man. I've seen him here before I think. He doesn't have a dog or anything so I suppose he just likes the park. Maybe he'd really like to go on the swings but he knows he's too old.

Mum's gone over to talk to Mrs Boots again. Oh, she's calling me over. I want to go on the American swings now. I love it when they get going but you have to push quite hard to get started. She's calling me and I go over to her. Mrs Boots looks at me and smiles. She's very pretty but not as nice as mum. Mum takes my hand and bends down to me. She tells me to keep away from the benches. I kind of look at her and she lifts her hand in that way that means DON'T ARGUE, so I say OK. Back to the American swings I go and then I see Eric running across the grass. He comes to the swing and plonks himself on the opposite side and we start it going. We don't say anything really but I'm glad he's there. He's bigger than me because he's in Primary Three with Miss Parker. I like playing with bigger boys because they do better things than little ones. Mum says I've really grown up this year and I feel really happy when she says that.

That man's still on the seat but the other two benches are empty. He's just kicked that girl's ball away. Usually, men kick it straight but he isn't a good kicker. He's turning to talk to her. Perhaps he's her grandpa and he's joking with her. It's funny because the women usually get fed up standing and go and sit. They can still keep an eye out because the benches are right next to the swings. Mum's moved along by the sandpit and is talking to another couple of women. Mrs Boots is going across there too. Ben is really pumping hard today and we're going backwards and forwards quite quickly now. He's standing up to get a better push but I'm not going to stand. I tell him to slow down but he's not looking at me and he keeps going. I'm OK though, I'm not too scared.

Just when we're really high and it's squeaking and shaking mum comes across and tells me we're going home. I'm quite glad really because Ben seems in a funny mood today as if he doesn't want to play. Mum takes my hand and we pass in front of the benches on the way out. We're pushing my little sister Kathleen, who's asleep as usual in her pushchair. I see the man has sunglasses on but there isn't any sun. He's got a funny straw hat on too. He doesn't turn to say hello or anything as we pass close but just stares straight ahead. He's probably thinking about something the way dad does sometimes.

Mrs Boots catches up with us pushing her kid in her pushchair. It's bigger than ours and has huge wheels. She says something to mum and they both turn to look at the man. She says she'll speak to someone. She says it's just not on and they both look at me in a funny way.

As we go out of the park, the woman who's our lolly-pop lady comes along with her husband. I think she's called Sheena. It's funny because she's really fat and he's long and thin. Mum says something to her and points over her shoulder. The lolly-pop lady shakes her head and laughs. She says that's Harry Mason and he's blind. Just likes to hear kids having a good time that's all. Mum says he's got no stick and Mrs Lolly-pop says he's got a foldaway one. I ask mum who's Harry Mason and she says 'Nobody darling, just my mistake.' Sometimes I think adults live on a different planet. How can a man be a mistake?

JUST ANOTHER DAY

He hasn't slept at all. He turns to the curtains and watches Superman become Superman again. For a second or two he forgets. He wants real things, not dreams. As he dresses she's back in his head and he shouts "Fuck off! Fuck-off!" to chase her away.

Downstairs, as he tries to eat his shredded-wheat, the day ahead comes: the green corridor he'll walk down, the banging doors, the kids shouting in the cloakroom, the drilling bells, the smell of onions from the dining room and that stare of Mrs Stone's. Thinking of these things comforts him, and he lets them settle. Then she's there again when he catches the smell of her pee at the foot of the stairs: there again, both hands clinging to his arm as they mounted the stairs last night, her legs floppy so she stumbled step by step. And she was giggling as she did with the gin, falling and giggling as if life was a joke and it wasn't, it wasn't, and he had to show her. At the top of the stairs, he'd pulled from her, away, free, and she left him. He hadn't thought she'd fall like that, over and over thumping and squealing to the bottom. Then she was quiet, her legs gone funny as if they'd been put on backwards.

Watching his spoon split the wheat, he feels his chest heave as if something inside him has been lifted. Inside comes out through his eyes. He doesn't often cry now and he feels stupid. He rubs and rubs his eyes as if that will clear things, stop his chest heaving. His spoon is shaking. He remembers the day his father left and how his mother and his sister laughed when he cried. They said he wasn't worth crying for, the bastard. Up on the wall, the Mickey-Mouse clock above the cooker is laughing.

The pain in his arm returns and he runs the cold tap over it till it goes numb and a different pain comes. He thinks of going up to her room again but he can't face seeing her lying there on her bed. He wonders what to do. His hand goes to his pocket and he feels the lump of notes he took from her purse. He's rich. There was a photo of him too but he ripped it up. He took seven pounds and some loose change before he caught sight of her open eyes in the dressing table mirror staring at him. It was as if she knew.

The house is quiet. His sister is sleeping-over at her friend's so there's not the usual noise from her radio, and none of the usual screaming from his mother that she wanted to sleep. The bathroom is empty. It's as if he's in another house. He showers to get rid of his mother's smell, washes his hair with his sister's special shampoo and sprays his armpits with his mother's deodorant. His pits smell of flowers. He feels clean, new, free: master of the house.

His father has been gone for over a year. It's as if he and his mother fell into the hole that he left - only his sister able to keep her balance. When his dad went, his sister called him a word his mother said she hated even more than she hated the old man. She only said it once but somehow from her lips, it sounded really bad. He remembers saying it twenty-odd times on his way to the bus that morning after his father left and each time it helped dry the tears.

He leaves the soggy remains in his bowl and an arc of pain sears his shoulders as he struggles to pull on his cagoule. He can still smell the pee from the hall. She must have done it when she landed.

Inside he's calm. Go to school as usual, he tells himself. He's lain all night wondering what to do but now he'll just go on as if nothing has happened. It's like the time he jumped the river with Marc and Tommy. He wanted in with them and one day he went with them to Marley's Wood where the river narrows and rushes between the old weir piles. They'd already jumped it, they said, and if he did, he'd be in. He didn't sleep the night before and after school they trooped up there. But when he stood, ready, he'd never felt so calm, so confident. He took a long run and sailed over, clearing it and only just gaining his balance. They hadn't even cheered or anything but as he squelched his way home he felt proud.

He feels that now, that calmness, that sense of defiance, wonders if he can go through the rest of his life doing things which other people are afraid to do. Maybe he can. He'll make a list of things sometime. He likes lists.

Outside the kitchen door, he swings his schoolbag at his mother's stupid wind chimes and they fly off their hook and clang like a bunch of musical sausages on the patio. It's drizzling now and the Crescent is stirring. A dog is on three legs against the lamp-post opposite Hussain's shop and Mr Hadden is loading ladders on to the roof of his van. It's just like any other day he tells himself, only better.

He catches the No 18 and arrives earlier than usual. Marc is kicking a tennis ball against the Girl's toilets and he joins in till the playground fills up and the bell goes. It's Friday - drama. He likes Miss Calder with her long blonde hair, the way the pony-tail swings when she turns suddenly. She's a good break from Mrs Stone. Some of the kids take the piss out of her and she struggles to keep control, but last week he'd acted a bus driver and she said she'd certainly ride on his bus someday and smiled at him and called him Joe. Today though, she seems tired and when Marianne throws a pen at Marc and hits him on the head, she goes crazy and screams. She isn't the same after that for the rest of the lesson and they don't do anything interesting.

Back in class after lunch, his mouth is rich with chocolate. Mrs Stone gets them writing. Once he wrote about Vikings coming to Glasgow. The class all laughed at the bit when they tore through The Buchanan Galleries and one of the raiders threw a security man over a balcony down three flights of stairs. Today though, they've to write about something they'd really like, that would change their lives. He starts writing about the iPod Marc brought to school on his birthday.

What I really want is a iPod. It costs a lot. It's a wee thing and you need a docking thing (don't know name) and then you set it up and it lights up and you can play your tunes. It's great. You get earphones too. All the time I could play music. That is what I would like.

He stops writing and looks up. His nose catches the scent of his flowery armpits then the cheesy smell of his trainers. He tucks his feet further under the table. Sarah Stewart's hair falls over her face as she writes, scribbling away then looking up for another idea. She uses words he's never heard of. She's always reading. Even when she goes on holiday, she told Mrs Stone she took piles of books to read and Stone said so did she and smiled. Marc's father has his own business and he gets everything he wants. Lucky bastard. He scrunches up his paper and starts again, driven by a fierce new anger.

What I'd like most is a mum and dad. Other kids have mums and dads but not all of them. Other kids have a stable home but not me. My mum's a drinker and Dad went away with his girlfriend. Good luck mum says but I liked him even if Mona didn't. Why can't everybody have a mum and dad that would be fairer and anyway if you want to change your life you've got to do it. I did it and now I don't know what happens if its care or what. Anyway, it's different now and I don't care.

Mrs Stone tells them all to stop writing, they'll read some of them out tomorrow. A man from the Gideon's is going to give them all a present in the hall in five minutes.

As he lifts his bag to put his jotter away, he feels a touch on his shoulder.

'Joe, what have you done to your arm?' He hadn't realised how far his shirt had ridden up in the fury of writing. The bruises look yellow under the lights of the classroom.

'Bumped it,' he says, and he doesn't look at her but continues packing.

'Joe. Look at me.'

'No,' he hears himself say.

'Stay behind Joe, I want a word.'

He looks up at her; that fat face, those little eyes that shine on some and go dead on others. All he sees in her eyes is anger because he's defied her. Now they've all gone quiet just looking at him. What does she care about him? What does she know about him? She's never liked him the way she likes kids like Sarah. Why should he give her anything? Why do what she says when he can defy her? Imagine Marc's face if he dared to...

'Fuck off!'

The words are out before he can crush them between thought and sound. She gasps.

'What did you say? Right, my lad.' Her eyes go mad and she rushes out of the room. The classroom goes quiet then becomes a buzz of voices. Marc looks at him like he did that time at the weir. Some of the others laugh and some turn away when he looks at them. In a moment, the class are told to leave and Mrs Stone comes back with the Head, Mrs Wilson.

As she speaks, he feels he's in a strange country whose language and gestures he doesn't understand. Here he is, Joe Mehan, alone with his teacher and the Head because of a sound he's made. He sees his mother's dead eyes, doesn't hear anything they say but pushes his desk away and barges his way out of the room. He runs now, past his class lining the corridor, past the Janitor's soapy cupboard and out the door into the playground.

He turns left outside the gate and makes for the woods. He passes mothers with prams, an old man carrying a plastic bag. He's sobbing as he runs, away and away from everything and everyone, even Marc's sneering face and he wonders what he'll think of him now. Told a teacher where to go. Other's kids had done it he knew. Bobby Graham in P7 had done it a year before and nothing much happened.

He flops, panting, below a tree and feels the wet leaves through his trousers. Doesn't matter now anyway does it? Who cares now? It's as if his world has moved, the way Stone told them about the Earth's Plates moving. He can feel the things inside him drifting about, shifting position as if nothing knows where it should be. It's not like this morning when he was still calm even with the tears. Now for the first time, a great fear clutches him and he begins to shake. He hears himself cry out over and over and the sound makes it feel better. Then there's a Tesco bag at his shoulder, and he feels a hand stroking him and stroking him like his mother's once did and his lips say 'Mum.'

KILLING THE MONKEY

His daughter had wanted him to stay for Christmas but he wouldn't have it, said he was on his own now, he'd be fine. So he walked slowly up the leaf-strewn path with his own case and his wife's little blue hospital case, aware of the fact that his legs weren't sure how to walk. Half-way up he thought he could hear a faint clacking, as if his wife's teeth were still trying to bite.

The house was dim, stinking of old carpet and dettol. She'd been sick a lot in the days before she went in to St Mary's and he'd become familiar with the red bucket under the sink. He closed the door behind him and noticed the mail on the mat; the usual supermarket bargains and local take-away menus. 'Flyers' they called this rubbish. He left it.

Upstairs in their bedroom, the branch that needed to be cut back tapped on the window. He opened the curtains a fraction and saw his daughter drive off, waving over her shoulder, though he knew she couldn't see him. The duvet was turned back on his side. Too big now then, the bed. He pulled back the duvet on her side, the dent still in her pillow, bent to sniff it. Some of her hairs were still there. Before and After played in his head now, a throbbing drum-beat that wouldn't stop and every part of the room joined in the chorus. It was the bed, the bed that sang loudest: it was where the distractions, the convenient separations of the days lost their currency and the strangeness between them grew like the last two dodgems, bumping, the scent of her always clinging as she twisted and turned, thumping the pillow, waking him with her moans lately as the pain increased. As the years passed, on those occasions when they went to bed at the same time, he'd tip his book and watch her undressing: that instinctive female choreography of top and bottom, inside and out, the gymnastics of arms and elbows, the snap of elastic, the roseate tracks on back and waist, the rolling, the lifting, then the dropping of the gown which once fell like a drape but latterly met resistance by middle-aged buttocks and thighs and he'd wonder at how little it stirred him. It was a scene from the play of their lives, one of the many devised by familiarity where habits were the script, where cues were taken or missed, though the plot didn't vary. He had never lost the memory of this bedroom as the place where the happy moments had been, but they were long gone. As he looked around the room he noticed how little it spoke of him.

The wallpaper was her choice, the pictures hers, the dresser drowned in a clutter of lacy mats, bottles, phials and little coloured bowls. There, like a dog drooling, glittery things dripped from the black-lacquered jewellery box she'd inherited from her grandmother. He didn't understand what those tongs with the curled ends were for or why she needed so many brushes each with different coloured bristles or why there were all those settings on the hair-dryer. The carpet by the dressing table was snowy with a stain of powder the shape of Africa and here and there on the carpet were spots where spilled medicine had congealed into little hard tufts.

He opened her wardrobe and in the chaos of blues and reds pulled out a hanger. A black shiny skirt hung from its thin loops like a giant bat. He threw it on the bed. He couldn't settle to anything, his head in turmoil, all focus gone. Then he remembered the monkey.

It didn't have a name. She'd had it as a girl and it had been with her ever since: a scrawny bald thing with one black eye and a curling tail. It was in her case. He clicked it open, pulled out her blue forget-me-not nighty, the pink cotton pyjamas, a cardigan, knickers, slippers, the toilet bag which rattled…and there it was.

'So you've come back have you?' he heard himself say. He lifted it, brought its mouth to his ear as she'd often done when they'd quarrelled as if this stuffed object were a friend to validate her case. 'Oh, you want to know where Mummy is, do you?' he said. 'Well, little monkey, Mummy isn't coming back. Mummy's left you and you've got me to look after you now. Isn't that good news!' He turned and caught sight of himself in the dressing table mirror. Some madman talking to a toy. His hand was shaking. He threw the creature on the floor and felt the head give under his shoe. Bewildered, he sat on the bed. He had to rid himself of her: all of her: smells, clothes, ornaments, words. He slapped out the impression still sharp on the crumpled bedsheets on her side then he pulled the sheets off the bed. Distracted again, he picked up the monkey and went downstairs.

In the kitchen cupboard, he found some green twine and made a noose which he placed round the creature's head. She wasn't coming back, the monkey's mummy: she wasn't ever coming back. He held the twine and let the monkey drop, disappointed that the twine didn't go taught. He searched for her sewing box, found a compartment with some pins. That was more like it. He lit the fire, made a cup of tea then taped the monkey where he could see it, from the rim of the up-lighter and stuck the final pin where its lost eye had been. Then another and another, feeling with each a release, as if the world were being put to rights, each pin a hurtful word, a rejection, a scornful look.

Half-an-hour later, he woke to a smell of burning. From the lamp, the monkey fell to the floor with a thump, the twine singed and smoking.

GRACE'S FAVOUR

Grace touched her daughter's moist little hand over her shoulder and watched in the mirror as she clambered out of the four-by-four and half-closed the door. She could never slam the heavy door properly. To hell with it. It would hold. It was eight forty-two. She was late.

She pulled out carefully into the flow of dropping-off traffic. Her heart was racing again and she realised she was gripping the steering wheel too tightly. She acknowledged Suzanne's mum's frantic waving in her little Clio and stopped at the lights. That old tramp with the long hair and the dog was crossing, as he seemed to every morning, the one Jack had always laughed at. She saw him most mornings at this time heading for the park. Now she thought there was something touching about the slow way he walked, the tilt of the head; the certainty of a life lived, as if nothing to come could shake him. She smiled, relieved that she still could. She wished for such calm, a peace to face the new day with hope. She was late.

"Any problems Mrs Archer?"

"Nuu…"

"Good. We'll just have a poke around and check things out."

Rubber fingers probed and he coded the state of her teeth to his assistant. The lamp loomed like something from E.T. She tried to hold herself in the moment: the eyes inches from hers; the feel of the tool scraping, pricking her gums; the expectation of pain; the sound of music somewhere; the swish of the assistant.

'Little chip off a filling up top. We'll make an appointment and put that right in no time.' At least this was life being lived. Something happening that had always happened...

He told her to swill out and she did so. She hated doing this now, having to spit in front of a man. There's no polite way of spitting. You just have to do it. It wasn't even like other bodily functions that you could control. My God, even farting you could control, but spitting - no - if you didn't spit heartily you were left with saliva drooling down your chin. She spat, wiped her mouth with the flimsy tissue and smiled as sedately as she could as the good-looking young man turned from his computer.

Grace drove the five miles to her semi in the suburbs. She sat at the table and ate a chocolate teacake left over from the previous evening. She watched the flakes of chocolate scatter on the table, licked her finger and dabbed them up to her mouth. The soft pine was scarred with gouges that Sophie had made doing her drawings and she traced them, felt her daughter's energy. Was it anger? A new wave of sadness crashed. A disintegrating cake for a disintegrating life.

Six months before, out of the blue, her husband announced he was leaving. She'd fought to keep him and he'd stayed. She learned his girlfriend had since left town and her little daughter still had a daddy.

At first, their "new start" had gone fine, but in time she noticed changes. He'd often touch her, even crossing the room to do it rather than the casual passing contact of previously, as if he felt the need to demonstrate affection. She'd lounge on the sofa with a book, her feet on his knees and feel his hands gently kneading her toes as he'd always done, but now it felt mechanical somehow. Was it because he rarely looked at her as he did it, she wondered? He wasn't idly, naturally, trying to give her pleasure, he was playing a part in the video of their previous life that had once been fresh and new and was now stale and disjointed.

It was as if he wasn't really there. He never seemed to be there those days, just going through the motions of family life like a marionette on strings. Every time she noticed his distracted look, it hurt. She bought him a pink jacket which he'd admired, in the hope that it might jolt him back to something like his old self, but eventually she was forced to recognise there was someone in his head sharing their life: someone who told him how handsome his white foam beard made him as he shaved; who ate with them so that he wouldn't hear her request for more wine; who made love with them, giving him a violent energy that frightened her. Then one day she said she wanted to talk.

She still remembered the look of terror on his face, but before she'd begun he'd turned to her and told her he was sorry, really sorry. It took her a second or two to realise that this wasn't an apology but a confession. As he began to sob, he told her the woman hadn't left after all and that he'd met her again at a meeting. He couldn't help himself - he loved her. She stared at this tear-filled stranger, then she laughed, as you'd laugh in shock as the blood wells from a cut, or at news that devastates beyond tears. She laughed and then she struck him across his face.

It was the end for them but for her it had been a beginning that led to nothing but an aching loneliness in a well of hurt. Her life seemed empty of its goodness, like the scooped and ridiculous shell of a grapefruit. Oh she wouldn't starve, and as to the house, well he'd had the nerve to make some joke about 'grace and favour.' 'It's rent free, but it's in my name, remember' he'd said as he walked away with two suitcases and a rucksack. For Sophie's sake, she didn't want to leave till the dust had settled. But what hurt most was the realisation that she'd been sharing her life with a ghost – a shade of once-love. Her daughter had cried every night for a week then found a new school friend. She saw her father every weekend and tonight she would stay with him and Grace would be alone again. A woman, a coffee and a teacake in this sunny, bleak, June.

The next morning her mood persisted but for the first time in two weeks she found the energy to do something. She'd been sleeping in the spare room since he left, unable to face their bed, the smell of him stronger than it had ever been. She'd removed some of her clothes and hung them in the little wardrobe, only going into her old bedroom for her make-up. Now she decided to clear out her wardrobe. She would get rid of clothes he'd liked, slough them off like a skin. Out went the red dress he'd given her one Christmas; out went the spotted blue one she'd worn to a wedding and thrown off later, as the wine and the moment took over; out went tops she associated with lunch at that French place; out went the coat he'd bought her when he'd been promoted; away went the stockings, the infernal garter belts, the scratchy knickers he bought her every Christmas.

As she bent to lift the pile of clothes at her feet, it was as if she were gathering leaves shed from an autumn tree. The light hangers clicked, but what hung now was authentically her. She bagged the clothes and drove to the Oxfam shop in the High Street.

The musty smell hit her immediately: one she had come to associate with virtue. You found it in churches cowering from a burning Italian sun, or here where the odour was of good intentions and old sweat. The woman thanked her and as she glanced round the shop, her eye caught a pink sleeve among the men's jackets. There couldn't be many jackets like that she thought. She lifted it down and opened it up. It was his. That sweet musk like a soaped armpit. There was no doubt, and yes, there it was - the tiny ink stain like the Isle of Wight on the inside pocket. It had driven him mad. He'd put a biro in there one day and it had leaked an island. As she closed the lapels, she couldn't resist the urge to put her hand in the pockets. It was as if she were peeking into a life after theirs. In the last pocket, deep in the breast pocket, she touched a piece of paper. She put it in her bag, replaced the jacket, and left the shop.

In the coffee shop next door, she felt the tension rise in her again. Why did she have to touch his damn jacket? It reeked of him. It had only started everything moving again that she wanted to stop. The natural process of grieving for a loss, yes even he, that bastard, was a loss. She'd given him trust, shared his intimate moments, cried helplessly in front of him, cared for him when he was ill and now they were strangers again - a cruel reversion. No, they were less than strangers, she decided. Strangers cause no pain. She thought of spinning objects in space that miss or glance or collide. They'd collided and she was still spinning from the blow.

She reached into her pocket intending to smell the piece of paper. She seemed hooked on scenting the past; she couldn't help herself. It was folded and there was a number on the pale green printer-paper. She knew it was local and it wasn't his new number: she'd insisted on knowing that when she'd agreed Sophie's weekend visits; she must be able to contact her daughter should anything happen. But she was sure there was never anyone else there. Sophie hadn't mentioned anyone else, despite subtle promptings. She put the slip of paper back in her pocket, shook herself, and went home.

'Hello?' A woman's voice. Peremptory.

'Oh hello, this is Oxfam in the High Street. I was given your number by Mr Jack Arfield. He told me to call you about a pink jacket that he's changed his mind about giving us. It's not our usual policy to allow customers to take back donations, but Mr Archer seems very concerned that there's been a mistake. He wondered if you could come in a pick it up. You'd have to buy it of course but we'll keep it aside.'

'Is this a joke?'

'I'm sorry?'

'I asked if this was a joke. Look, for a start, anyone who'd want to wear that bloody jacket deserves all they get, and secondly, Mr Archer as you so politely call him, can get lost, if he thinks I'm going to Oxfam to retrieve it. You can burn the bloody thing for all I care. Now if you don't mind, I have a client in five minutes…'

'Thanks for your time. Sorry to bother you. I'll let Mr Archer know you're not able to help. Goodbye.'

She put down the phone. Her hands were shaking but she felt triumphant in a way she couldn't define exactly. Was that her? Was that the bitch that had ruined their life? If it was, things seemed a bit rough on the domestic front. She heard a voice in his ear saying 'Get rid of that jacket. I suppose she bought it, did she?' Then it struck her. In three days time, he would be taking Sophie to school as he always did on a Monday…

'Bye darling. Now don't slam the door, it's not like Mummy's car. Everything's fine. It'll just be the two of us again on Saturday, and remember don't say anything to Mummy.' The door of the Mercedes shut soundlessly.

'Can't be easy said his partner Bill.'

As he moved off into the stream of dropping–off traffic, the lights ahead changed to red. To his left, waiting to cross was the old man.

'That old guys a bit sharp isn't he Jack. Like the jacket,' said Bill.

Crossing the road with a nonchalance that defied his years and status, the tramp sported his new pink jacket.

SOFT SOAP AND DISHES BEST SERVED COLD

Two years of clanking locks, shouts thin as a blade, the sun's dimpled shadows through the suicide netting of B - hall. Tomorrow I'm out. No more pictures, just the real you, Julie…

Everything shimmered in the noon heat, making the little yellow loading- trucks and their blue workers sway like drunks. Mad dogs and Scotsmen time, it felt, for I'd forgotten what heat was, my eyes and skin dulled from a grey London March. Driving from the airport in Malaga at noon, snaking my way into the traffic heading West, the backs of my knees burned against the plastic piping of the seat. Sun. Heat. I'd forgotten the blessing. Hoardings flanked the road advertising Sun-Golf and Golf-World. How about Dickhead Golf and Pratt Golf, I thought, at that moment hating the whole Pringle-pullovered crowd that my old man felt so at home with.

Between the hoardings, the grey knuckles of the mountains gleamed when the mist lifted and I thought of the gorilla of a bloke who'd rung my bell two days before, the way he'd caressed his fists, the way his bracelet chuckled.

My bottles rattled with every gear change, the stick fighting my wrist and the Clio's little engine growling, abused by a succession of hire-car Brits. I'd been told to take the exit before Fuengirola. I'd been here before but that was with her and she knew it all well. Now as I braked to allow a red BMW into my lane from the slip-road, I wondered what she would be doing in her cosy English Country-House. At least it would be green, not this blue-brown hopelessness. The thought of her brought her voice, clear as then, its chill steel ripping into me once too often. She'd grabbed one of my tea-towels to stop the bleeding and the last I'd heard was her heels' tattoo on the stairs.

I caught my exit and climbed the steep hill through ranks of little villas, growing in size with the gradient. You pay more for cooler air. White walls, exotic trees and pools. That was all this was - boredom with a long shadow.

I stopped at the black gate in a wall. Only the white chimney stack was visible behind. I rang the bell and soon a middle-aged woman appeared.

'Hi. Tom. I think you're expecting me?'

'I'm Sue. Come in, won't you.'

She led me down a steep flight of red-tiled steps, her floral backside rolling, Inside it was cool, and she showed me round saying her husband was out working but he'd be back soon. I unpacked and took one of the bottles out to the table on the patio.

The little valley was spread out below me and I could see the sprawl of Fuengirola's tower blocks, hazy in the distance like some sick joke played by the tide. It was March but the sun was as hot as August in London. A dog barked nearby and then an answering bark rasped from across the way. I fingered the package in my pocket for the tenth time that day. I'd been shitting myself that the machine would pick something up. Nothing. I passed through the gate struggling to keep calm. This was my passport to happiness, the Greek had told me, and I had to believe him.

I'd tried to remember the address but I was tired now and I'd forgotten it. Calle de Toro. The bull plaque. It was money. Up there in Mijas just waiting for me and how I needed it. Too many horses with three legs. I couldn't see the town from here, but at the thought of it, I tasted that gazpacho from her spoon and saw that blue butterfly that fell in love with her hat. It was our first holiday together and I'd believed that the villa was owned by a friend of her father. She'd seemed so happy the first few days then insisted that we went for a ride in a horse-drawn carriage through the narrow white streets. I'd felt embarrassed, West-coast Scotsman doing the ultra-tourist thing: imagined the sun-wizened driver having a laugh. We'd fallen out that night and words said had bitten deep.

When I found out that it was her father's villa I couldn't believe it. He was a shopkeeper, a small kind-faced little man with a huge moustache and a big smile. He owned a small hardware shop and I couldn't work out how he could own such a house. And the two guys that seemed to hover. Who the hell were they? I imagined a nice little place for two and here we were in a twelve-room mansion with servants around every bend. That night she let slip that the way she spoke, that street-cred patter, was as false as her nails. She'd been educated at Roedean. It wasn't till we got back to London and the big Cypriot bruiser paid me a visit that the pigeons came home to roost. Archbishop Makarios had heard from a little bird that Miss Julie was very unhappy and his eyes promised untold suffering should I misread the earnestness of his words. Now Julie's old man wanted a little favour…

As the Ardbeg's peaty music danced in my throat, I closed my eyes and listened. Somewhere between the chirping birds, the occasional dog and the hum of the pool's heating system on the level below, there came the just audible moans of human pleasure. I smiled at the thought that not far away someone was having a good time.

Later that evening I met Phil, the owner, Sue's man. The villa had been run down for one reason or another and being a plumber to trade he'd had the know-how to take it on. He said he knew Julie's father from way back, hoped I'd find the house OK. After the offer of a whisky which he declined, he went back up the steps to his own apartment which was guarded by three Great Danes. Soft as putty they are, he said, and I said right. More bouncers.

The next morning I drove up to Mijas, parked at the less touristy end and walked through the narrow white streets up to her father's house. I thought of Julie again, her slim legs solid through that white dress when the sun caught it. I'd imagined every guy we passed having his own little fantasy and remembered the shiver of pride that only I could live it. We learn. A mangy black cat glanced at me and scurried away as if it knew something I didn't. I rang the bell.

A red-headed maid led me into the conservatory overlooking the valley. Mr Wallace would be with me in a moment. My heart was racing so I sat in a cane chair and tried to calm down. Just be professional, I told myself. This is business. He's expecting you. He knows what you'll say and you know what he'll say. Stay loose. I picked up an African carving and felt it cool in my palms. It was new. There was laughter somewhere; a mocking laughter I thought, then convinced myself it was only my imagination. I heard footsteps and looked up to see Julie standing in the doorway, her hand draped over the handle.

'Tom. Great to see you again. How are you?'

'Julie. I wasn't expecting…'

'Oh don't look so sheepish. There's no damage done. Let's just put it down to a little anger management problem shall we?'

She was tanned and was wearing cut-off jeans and a white blouse tied under her breasts. She looked so at home I couldn't relate this woman to the shy girl who'd asked me if I thought it would be cold up there in Mijas. What a clown I was. I took it all in. She must have been enjoying every moment. And the voice was back: the posh voice had come home.

'Look, I don't know what's going on here. I came to deliver something and then I'd be paid.'

'Of course you did. Have you got it?'

'It's for your father.'

'It's for me, actually. Drink?'

'No thanks. Look I don't suppose it matters as long as I get paid. Have you my money?'

She poured herself a drink and sat opposite, crossing her tanned legs a little more slowly than necessary. I thought of Basic Instinct then I thought of Kenny Everett and smiled.

'Share it.'

'Sorry?'

'The joke.'

' I feel like I'm in the middle of some surreal movie or something when nothing is as it seems. It's a bit confusing, that's all. Do you have my money or not?'

'I have you.'

'What?'

'I have you. Open it.'

I was beginning to feel out of my depth here. This woman I'd fought with and slapped and whom I didn't expect to see ever again was now sitting opposite me in her father's house with God knows how many goons in the building and she was beginning to sound as if revenge was the main dish on the menu. My mate Patrick's advice kicked in – at the first hint of danger, make provision. "Make provision." My provision was to remember the way out and to get the hell out of here if things got any stickier.

'The package?'

'Where's your father? Zorba the Greek said it was for your father.'

She turned and shook a little bell on the table next to her. I knew it wasn't for dinner and a chill coursed through me like the time I'd been surrounded in the woods once. Three older boys, one of whom I'd slapped for slagging off my sister. I shifted and prepared to respond quickly.

Two men in dark suits appeared at the door and moved behind Julie.

'Show Mr Burns to his room gentlemen. I'm sure he'd like to relax.'

I nodded in assent and followed them down the corridor still half-believing that Julie's old man would eventually appear. Halfway down the guy in front swivelled. I glimpsed a fist before the black swept over me.

I woke later, dragged into consciousness by a jaw twice normal size and a custard made of iron-filings in my mouth. There was a towel under my head to absorb my bleeding and I wiped my mouth with it as I moved towards the window. I was high up and the whole valley seemed shrunken and misty below. The window was locked shut. I washed in a small sink and stared at myself in the mirror. I looked but refused to think about what I saw. There were more pressing considerations than my appearance. I sniffed. I'd pissed myself.

They kept me there for two days only allowing me out to crap and piss in the bathroom next door. One of them had to be restrained from having another go at my jaw when I asked if we could come to an arrangement.

After two days Julie appeared again. Her father was with her this time and he did the talking.

'You disappoint me, Mr Burns. I welcomed you into my family and you abused my daughter. I cannot accept that. You brought the soap a long way. I thought some cleansing agent appropriate for the cleansing of sin. Clever isn't it? Julie assured me you'd be greedy enough to be taken in. Now that you've paid in some way for your disrespect I think we are even don't you? Oh and just so that you don't bear any grudges I'm going to give you another little package which Georgios will collect in London. You'll be well paid of course.'

I took the package, same size and weight as the last one and put it in my bag. Soft soap the bastards, get free.

As I passed through Heathrow they grabbed me. 'Interesting package sir. Perhaps you'd like to step this way…'

I've become an artist, in case I forget her face…

BASHED NOSES AND BROKEN DREAMS

Honest Jill, he's watching the football and I hear the kid screaming and I go through and he's got a hold of her hair and he's going I'm really sorry darling it's just a tug. The lassie's bawling her eyes out and every time she pulls away it gets worse. Leave her alone I'm shouting and he gets up and gives me one of those looks. I'm scared Jill, I really am. Poor wee soul was in agony but she's so loyal she'll always make an excuse for him… It was a tuggy Mum. Dad got it stuck… you know the sort of thing. Clumsy bugger.

You wouldny believe half the things he does Jill, you really wouldny. Canny believe that was the bloke I married ten years ago… Squeezed a few quid out of him this morning. He's feeling bad about Emma see, so it's an open-wallet situation, if you get my drift.

Where was I? Oh aye, you know who. Folk change, don't they? He was okay when I met him. Quite kind, really. Wouldny let me pay for anything. He was playing for the Hibs then and I'd go and watch him. You'll no credit it, but he'd my name tattooed on his arm in these big Chinky-looking letters. So, here's me sitting with all these folk in the stand and he scores a goal and he looks up to the stand, pulls up his shirt and points at his arm. And he's pointing to my name! Y-v-o-n-n-e. My God, I couldny get over it. No that I like football, but when your bloke's a hero like that, it's a big buzz. God, I can remember some of the things we did in those days before he went on the buses and had the accident… I'm sure I must've told you about that time in Watson's back shop. Anyhow, old Watson was out doing a delivery to that old woman with the wee Pekinese dog, and who comes marching into the shop bold as brass but our hero. We'd been going out for a few weeks and getting on great. Well he didny like me talking about other blokes mind you and it wasny as if he'd never had girlfriends… Anyhow, I'm there in the shop and he's standing there in this Hibees track top still sweaty from training and I was really surprised to see him and I says do you want to see the back shop, thinking I'd get him out the way if Watty came back. God was I green about the lugs to come out with something like that! Red rag tae a bull if you know what I mean, Jill. So in we go and I'm hardly through the blinking door when he grabs me and flings me against the wall. Honest Jill, I know I shouldny go on about it but my God I've never had it like that in my life. And we'd just… you know… finished, when the door opens and Watty's standing there with this look on his face and we all freeze and he says 'I'd like a word Yvonne.' Adios amigo! Och he was a nice man really. I suppose you canny blame him for giving me my books. Must've been a sight for sore eyes seeing me with my knickers round one leg and the colour of a tomato. Oh, and the funniest thing was, just as you-know-who was leaving the shop the old boy shouts out 'You'll no be doing any more scoring this week then!' It was quite funny really. Anyhow, there's been loads of scummy water under the bridge since then. I've had him up to here, I really have, and I want out. That bairn's going to be traumatised if this goes on much longer. Canny tell from one moment to the next what mood he's going to be in and it's doing my head in, it really is Jill.

Don't look now, but there's a very fit-looking item up at the bar over there. No! Christmas, I said don't look, and you just turn and look! You know what they're like: one wee bit of eye-contact and they're on you. If your luck's in, that is. Don't think he clocked you looking. God, he's nice though. Hugh Grant type with floppy hair. What? Och, come off it Jill. I did it once and that hardly makes me a scarlet woman. If it comes to that, I've seen your eyes on their stalks before now, so don't come the Mother Theresa with me. Seriously though, it's funny how you're never really bothered most of the time. Celebrities and movie stars and that, goes without saying, but apart from Robbie Williams and the gorgeous Brad, I'm no really bothered, ken? Tend to go for the good-looking ones. I'm no really into the Steve McQueen type with the bashed noses and that, like that guy what's his name… Craig, the new James Bond. No, give me a guy with regular features anytime. Connery? Don't get ma juices running Jill. That man's a pure doll. Christ what age is he now, about ninety- three and he's still gorgeous. Funny though, how you dream about these guys but it doesny really matter if you're happy. If I'm at home with wee Emma and he's at the pub or at the Centre, I couldny be happier. Just me and her and a box of After-eight mints and a video she likes. I'd do anything for that wee soul I really would.

Sometimes I go into her room and she's lying there with no duvet on and I just look at those wee legs all curled up and the hair over her eyes and I canny believe she's mine. She's my whole world. I just love her to bits. Seems like the more I love her, the less I like him though. He's her father, but I don't think he cares a flying thingy about her. Football and drinking's all he cares about. You're lucky Jill, Tommy's still crazy about you. No, don't deny it, he is.

He did what? You're kidding! And was it nice? Mine wouldny have the gumption for that kind of thing. I went to an Ann Summers once and I couldny help laughing at all thon stuff. They giant willies that do a wee dance when you press a button. Yuk! Did I tell you I tried on one of those basque things in the bedroom. Honest Jill, I looked in the mirror and I couldny believe it was me. I was spilling out all over the place and these suspenders were dangling down everywhere. God, it wasny half itchy! I remember the woman demonstrator knocked at the door and came in and she looks at me and says You look gorgeous Margaret, and I says Well I feel like a whore and my names Yvonne actually. I didny take to her early on and I just couldny be bothered with any more of her sales-pitch. Stupid bitch. You should've seen her face, it was a picture. No, I'm no into that sex- toy stuff I have to say. Anyhow, why would I want to get him all hot and bothered when I canny stand the bugger. Sunday morning's bad enough. Oh Jill, you're a woman, you know. You wake up and look at the clock and you can hear him snoring and you think I'll get up and do something, just to get out of the bed. Then while you're thinking about it you hear this fart and then he's awake and you know what's coming next. I know I shouldny be telling you all this Jill, you'll have your own problems, but honest, I've nobody else to talk to. You know what it's like when you're no in the mood but they start pawing you and nuzzling into you like they do and you feel you just canny refuse. Honest to God, I lie there and let him do it just to get a bit of peace for Emma's sake. Doesny last long anyhow, thank God. No these days. See the mood if he doesny get it though! That stale breath on your face and he's trying to kiss you for God's sake. Most of the time I just cut off and I lie there wondering whether I've got enough Coco Pops for Emma. Christ maybe it's our lot, just to put up with it. Women's lib, aye that'll be right! I remember my mother telling me one day that marriage would be great in some ways and no so great in others. She looked at me in a funny way as if I was supposed to know what she was getting at but to be honest I couldny see past those green eyes then. That was when I was having Emma and I felt like the bees knees. I really did. Wasny even sick. Just this ginormous belly and folk saying he'd be a footballer like his dad. My dad never liked him. Mind you, I suppose no father likes the idea of another man getting their hands on their wee girl. Anyhow Jill, by the time

Emma's courting, there'll be no father to fight off her boyfriends. I'm going, I really am. No, don't laugh. I know it's no the first time I've said it, but this time, I really am. I've written to my auntie Jean in Kinghorn and asked if I could stay with her for a wee while to get on my feet. Told her I'd had enough of him.

My mum? I wouldny get much of a welcome there. You'd think your own mother would back you up when you needed a wee bit of comfort even if she wasny your biological one. Forget it. All I get is, 'Well Yvonne I have to be honest, I don't think you're blameless in all this.' Christ, with the old pan loaf too. She always talks like that on the phone or when she's on her high horse. The words slow right down and come out as if she's the source of all wisdom or something. My real mother would've backed me to the hilt but no thon sour puss. No, she wasny always like that. Aye okay, I know. It was a mistake. I shouldny have done it, but I was really lonely and Billy was nice to me. Och, come on Jill, don't give us the face. I told him the truth when it went too far. Aye, I know it wasn't easy for Jim - it wasn't exactly easy for me either you know. You're supposed to be my friend, right? Sorry, but I thought pals were supposed to be there for you when you need them. Oh aye, okay, I 'll give you that. It was hard for him when he had the accident, but I had a bairn to look after and a man with one leg. He was always under my feet too, going on and on about why him, what had he done to deserve this. Remember that holiday when Tommy and you came with us to Ibiza, after the accident? If only I had some of that compensation cash now, but it doesny bring back your leg does it? Anyhow, remember that trip on the boat to thon island? What a day that was, and that guy, the Rep guy, God, he was something else! Just as well Jim wasny there or I'd've had my backside skelped. Emma? No, she was ill, remember. He stayed with her at the hotel. He couldn't get around much anyhow. But what a terrific day! Oh, that's right, we went back and the wee soul was splashing about in the pool and thon old biddie, the one with the pearls telling him that Emma shouldny be in the pool with all the muck that was floating in it. It was a bloody disgrace that, right enough, after what we paid. Next day he wouldny let her in and the wee soul was crying her eyes out, and me and him had that rammy. Well, Jill, I couldny see the problem. What was the harm in letting the kid have a wee paddle? Are you going already? It's just after six…

I told him I was away to the pictures so he'll no expect me back till nine-ish. Och well, if you're off you're off. Anyhow, I'll let you know what happens. Aye sure, I'll give him your love okay. Good old Jim. Jill loves you. Glad somebody does.

THE CAMEL COAT

She said he'd enjoy it. What he needed was a bit of culture, take his mind off making money. It was his first concert, Bach's Cello Suite in G major and it was the same music that played when his Chess-master computer programme kicked in. He could see the flashy chess pieces levitating in bubbles. Chess was culture, wasn't it? But he was bored. He called up his toes and wiggled them to make sure they were still there. He flexed each thigh then sat up straight till he felt an ache at the back of his neck. His nose was full of her perfume and he turned to see her narrow hand resting on her lap, its nails manicured and carmine, a red hair on her white silk cuff. Silk cut. His wife Evelyn's hair was black. He couldn't stop comparing her to Evelyn. Something as seemingly insignificant as the colour of a hair summed up the excitement of what he was doing. Hair was so intimate. He'd loved watching her brushing it before they left; sitting where Evelyn sat, on that plush stool, her hair beginning to shine as if the shine was coming out of the brush. The piano rose and the cello answered. Its sonorous tone reached him low down and he realised he needed to pee. Should have gone before it started but they'd been in a rush. He remembered their earlier conversation:

'Your body is beautiful.'
'I suppose it is.'
He'd laughed.
'Why are you laughing?'

'Oh, nothing. It's just that when you pay someone a compliment, you sort of expect them to disagree, to be humble about it in some way.'

'Sorry. No, my body isn't beautiful. It's pretty ugly. I don't know how you can bear to lie on top of me. Is that better?'

'Don't be silly. You know what I meant.'

'When did you first think my body was beautiful?'

'When? The first time I saw you.'

'But you didn't really see my body then.'

The conversation wandered through corridors papered with ego and mock hurt. She had that ability most women have, to spin webs of words that bind men's tongues. Of course, she was helped by his adoration. But she was teasing. All the time she teased while he thought he had hurt her feelings. She was perched on a hill and he was always looking up. In the end, he saw she detected his anxiety and stopped playing by placing her hand round his cock. He smiled, reassured, but inside, he began to fear her. She knew how to play him. His bladder interrupted his reverie.

By the end of the concert he walked to the toilet with a supreme effort of self-control. She was waiting for him outside, talking to a man in an expensive looking camel coat who quickly disappeared when he noticed Graham was returning. Did she tip him the wink?

'Hi. Who he?' Better a jokey approach than to show any jealousy.

'He friend.' There was punctuation in her eyes and it was a full stop.

The car was freezing. A light snow had started to fall and was beginning to powder the streets. He drove her to the usual place at the corner of a street of terraced houses. She'd walk the rest she said. She'd said that every time but he hadn't pushed things. He wouldn't push the hubby button just yet. She said it had been a great evening and she'd give him a buzz.

The Camel Coat

He'd met her at the business networking breakfast in a crummy hotel. All those tables: the baskets with the flaky greasy croissants, the orange juice, the stiff, cold, little butter parcels, the men and women in suits at seven o'clock in the morning baggy-eyed but eager, ready to chat and share names and addresses: the needy meeting the needy.

'Do you know Tara Fears, Graham? Everyone knows our Tara. For obvious reasons, I have to say. But a damn good lawyer too.'

'That's enough of that, Jim. "Everyone knows our Tara" makes me sound like the town whore or something. We meet again, Graham. I'll try not to spill my coffee on your shoes. Don't think I've seen you here before have I?'

'No. First time. Not my scene really, all this glad-handing stuff.' She was beautiful. He'd bumped into her at Taylor and Reid's when she'd spilled some files at his feet. She stood out like a cut thumb on a cold day. Long red hair, grey fitted suit, long blue legs. No ring.

And that was it. He got her extension and rang her two days later. Why not? He was free. He was sure she was married but he didn't care: if she said yes, great, if no, fine. But he was lonely. They went for dinner. Polite sparring but nothing deep, then back to his place. He was aware of her eyes everywhere: questions about his DVD'S, a quick stroke of a Chinese lamp, a kitchen survey, questions about him. She did all the talking, he realised afterwards, a little fearful that he might not be her type - not assertive enough. She skyped him the next night.

With Bach still in her ears, Tara walked up the steps to her door. Jude Fears lay sprawled in an armchair, a gin in his hand. No sign of Irma, the au pair.

'Irma's just gone through. She sat watching some film with Lewis. He couldn't sleep. Came in and there was the pair of them wrapped in the blanket. Very cosy. That was a close thing. Do you think he twigged?' He could see the swell of her buttocks under the tight skirt as she bent over the sink to fill a glass with water. She seemed quiet tonight.

He tipped back his gin, sucked on the lemon slice and sat down deeper in the leather armchair, the empty glass still in his hand. He was still in his expensive cashmere coat, bought on a whim after a rare win on the horses. There was no sound from the other room, so he assumed the child was asleep. He'd checked the result on his phone. They'd won 3-1. Wow. They never won, but he'd taken a punt. He felt for the thin betting slip in the pocket of his coat. Was reassured. Things were looking up. He took off the coat and threw it over the armchair. He moved to her and placed his hands on her hips. 'I'm not in the mood, Jude. You go to bed. I need to wind down for a bit.' He kissed her neck and left, stopping to listen outside Irma's door for a moment to hear her gentle breathing. A lovely girl, Irma, he mused. Perhaps…

Tara Fears had been in her office when she'd seen Goodman emerging from one of the Associates' rooms. She recognised him from a piece she'd read in the paper about his marital problems. No oil painting, she'd thought, and in the same moment a picture of her own man, fat balding Jude, had supplanted it. She smiled. In a bar in the centre of town, she saw Goodman again, talking with a woman. She found herself fascinated by this tall fair-haired man who'd made so much of his old man's legacy and yet was at the mercy of his wife. She'd seen Evelyn Goodman at functions: slim, black straight hair, but too much make-up on one of those blunt working-class faces that could never be beautiful. It was her eyes that gave her away though, that dead look that tells you there's no-one in. Tara looked down at her hands and tried to remember the last time she'd had a manicure. Jude, the lovely Jude, had a bad habit of misplacing money and it tended to be her money that he lost on horses, dogs and football. She was pissed off with the scrounger yet she loved him. Something about the way he smiled when he'd tell her he'd had more bad luck. He had always lived on the edge and at first she'd loved

The Camel Coat

the danger, but now, forty-three, and her future in the firm threatened by his reputation, she needed to change things. She knew she was still attractive, could draw looks from much younger men when she allowed herself to walk the walk and talk the talk. If somehow she could get closer to Goodman, who knows where it might lead, what little gifts she might receive? She'd broached the possibility with Jude and he'd stormed off. Two days later he said he'd agree because he loved her. Only because he loved her and it would help little Lewis.For Tara however, the prospect of being a rich lady without Jude tickled somewhere deep.

Two days later she dropped some files at Goodman's feet and they began to talk.

Three days later they met at the networking breakfast.

Outside Goodman's window, the snow was still falling and it occurred to him that it might affect construction work on the new hospital. He'd pulled off the contract despite stiff opposition from two other local contractors - the result of playing golf with councillor McLeod and missing a few easy putts.

Goodman had taken over his father's business and through luck and good judgement had made it stronger than the old man would ever have imagined. Now he was comfortably set, with a large house and a portfolio of shares that grew by the minute, it seemed. He stared out at the headland and felt that life had been good to him but with his wife's departure he now stood to lose half of everything he'd built up.

Evelyn and he had been happy together till the business began to grow and Goodman found himself spending more and more time working. Never a resourceful woman, she'd become bored and lonely and had sought company with a group of old college friends amongst whom was Lenny Fraser, a young solicitor. An old story and one that never ends. She'd come clean about the affair and Goodman had slapped her hard. He loved her and she stayed for a bit, but things were never the same between them and she told him one day that she wanted a divorce. They'd discuss things later, he said, hoping that she'd disappear from his life. He couldn't talk about it. He never could find the right words when emotions filled him. He'd stutter and shake and end up just staring as his lips trembled. After all, she was the unfaithful one. The solicitor's letters (not Fraser's, but who knows what connections he would have) were polite at first, but as Goodman stalled, they became increasingly threatening. He contacted his own man, but it didn't look good from a financial point of view. Goodman missed his daughters, whose departure he had reluctantly agreed to, but couldn't reconcile himself to losing a couple of million pounds as well. Now he'd met Tara and wanted to wipe the slate clean with Evelyn.

The house's dark had greeted him as it usually did these days, rebuking him as a failure as a husband. He was left with emptiness and silence while Evelyn had her new man and the children. He was tired and yet he knew he wouldn't sleep. Night after night he'd lain trying to sleep and yet his brain wouldn't rest, forever gnawing away at his situation. Now he'd fallen into the routine of getting up at three or four and padding down the stairs to watch some God-forsaken Open University programme on what causes drought in India or how genetically modified crops might turn us all into freaks. Sitting freezing in his dressing gown, a mug of milkless tea in his hand and the screen flickering, he imagined Tara appearing naked at the top of the stairs like one of Canova's Three Graces in that postcard she'd shown him. He felt such desire, his throat gone dry and his heart thumping while she smiled down on him before moving away trailing her eyes like some silk chemise. He knew he was in thrall to her and he knew it wasn't good. There was something he couldn't touch about her, something just out of reach, and he had recently begun to feel it might never be within reach. As with Evelyn, he became conscious that he was being led rather than leading: he knew more clearly what he feared than what would make him happy.

Nothing was said about the husband and Goldman hadn't wanted to push a button that might detonate a blast of unpleasant talk in the midst of fleshly delight. He couldn't help thinking about the man in the camel coat though and how intimate their conversation seemed. Was that him? If that was him, why the secrecy; why couldn't she just say 'That's the bastard I married and I hate the sight of him.' The old fear kicked in. They'd been together for a month but there'd been no invitation to her home. In fact, her home hadn't been mentioned; just that this was her street and how lovely she thought his house was. Then he had the idea to Skype her as she had him: he wanted to see her, wanted her face to allay all his fears. He was being paranoid. Of course Tara loved him. These paranoid thoughts were his wife's legacy.

He dialled her up and after a couple of minutes, her face appeared on his screen, slightly distorted as if she were only pretending to be Tara but failing.

'Graham,' Then she leaned forward and tried to whisper 'Are you mad? I wasn't expecting this.'

'You skyped me, didn't you?'

'Yes, but you're free. I've still got….you know.' She half-turned over her shoulder.

'Are you missing me already?' The words came from her lips as if she were a ventriloquist's dummy; as if some malicious force manipulated her. That sneering tone that he detested had kicked in quickly. Teasing him, as if he were a dog or something. He didn't reply for a few seconds. Let her stew in her words, he thought. Let her hear what she sounds like, the beautiful bitch. It was then that he glanced over her right shoulder into the visible segment of the room and spotted a garment draped across a chair. A camel-coloured garment. The picture wasn't great, but the colour was unmistakable.

'I see hubby's left his coat on the chair. Did he enjoy the concert? You're becoming careless Tara.'

'Sorry?'

'I'll bet you are.'

'Graham, what are you talking about?' She turned round. 'That's a blanket.'

For a moment he was unsettled, then he told her to lift it up and show him.

'I bloody well will not. What is this, a fashion parade or an inquisition? Just go to bed Graham, you're becoming delusional. It was a lovely evening. I'll ring you tomorrow.'

'Don't bother Tara. I don't know what's going on but there's a strong smell of rodent in the air.'

He switched off and sat, immobile for a minute, his words still hot on his lips. 'Don't bother,' he'd said. So simple, so right, and yet the loneliness he'd felt when Evelyn left hit him even harder now: every chair, every photograph his eyes rested on screamed the emptiness of his life. He went to bed and lay sleepless and desperate till the faint light of a new day lit the curtains. There was snow on the lawn and the pond looked to have frozen over, yet inside he felt that something dangerous and minatory had been doused. All the time he'd been with Tara, he'd felt uneasy, and the more he untangled the reasons, the more sure he became about himself. He realised she was a symptom, not a solution; that in her looks and intelligence he found everything that Evelyn lacked but it was he, Graham Goodman, who was lacking really, to tie himself to women who seemed to dominate him so easily.

She rang him three times over the next week but he fought the urge to respond. Then the week following he saw her in a bar sitting with a young woman and a child. She looked as beautiful as ever, laughing, that red hair tied back in a green scarf, her delicate hands cradling a cup. Not much to indicate that she was missing him. He felt a strong impulse to face her, to confront her with his anger, but something stopped him. This time, it wasn't fear. He

The Camel Coat

knew her now; knew what made her tick and what he knew made him cold. He didn't care now. Let her play her games on someone else. Then he stopped and turned back, confused by a heart that thundered in his chest.

Inside the cafe, she waved and came across to him, a look of mock apology on her face.

'Graham. What a fuss over an old blanket. I've missed you so much.'

He took her hand and kissed it. Only then did he notice the colour of her coat draped over her chair.

JAKUB'S ANGEL

Jakub Pasternak was not a handsome man. Jakub wasn't even ugly, for that can have its own attractions so women tell us. His friend Mal once called him "neep-heid" and Jakub laughed at the unusual sounds and Mal laughed too, before explaining what a neep was. Though Jakub's face was large and featureless, its landscape was enlivened by his smile. Mal thought there might just be hope for him yet with some woman, but said nothing.

Jakub was twenty-three years old and had worked in the post office in Krakow but along with many of his countrymen, he experienced an irresistible urge to move West in search of a better life. After an unhappy few months in London, he took a train North and three weeks after that he was behind the wheel of a number 22 bus driving through the centre of Edinburgh to the Ocean Terminal at Leith.

One hot June day his attention wavered and he ran down a cyclist on Leith Walk. Although the young man recovered, for Jakub it was a turning point: all the frustrations and boredom that had been building in him seemed relieved as he emptied his locker.

Two weeks later he met a man in a pub who worked in the National Gallery. They were looking for a bit of diversity in their staff he said. Jakub had always liked pictures, though his experience of them was confined to table mats and the occasional print that he'd come across in someone's flat. The idea of visiting a gallery had never occurred to him any more than the thought of visiting the Botanic Gardens would have, but now he applied and got the job as an assistant in the National Gallery, at Mal's suggestion, telling the bald smiling man who interviewed him that he'd always liked art, particularly Jack Vettriano's pictures. The man looked at him and a weak smile crossed his face. Jakub feared the worst, but in a few days, he learned he had got the job.

Now, ensconced in the Victorian plum-tinted splendour of the National Gallery of Scotland, he sat and planted his shiny shoes and felt an incredible itch in his anus. He knew scratching was impossible so he clenched his teeth and the itch faded. There was an earpiece in one of his ears for any alarms and he was dressed in his new dark green Gallery-tartan trews with the three thin red stripes – signifying the three Galleries. He felt smart and important and he was upstairs in the little rooms with the Impressionists.

It was a Tuesday morning and by the umbrellas, he knew it was raining in Princes Street. Opposite and just along from where he sat there was a portrait of a fat man called Martelli by Edgar Degas and to the right was Gauguin's "Vision of the Sermon." He liked the idea that this was another Jakub doing a bit of wrestling though he hadn't ever thought of angels as being particularly interested in wrestling. Surely angels being such good creatures would always let you win. He couldn't imagine an angel throwing you down and stamping on you then turning to the crowd with a raised fist or wing or something and going Yeeeeeeeeah!

Such thoughts filled his head as a thin trickle of "the public" wandered through his room. They were a mixed bag: some foreign tourists with see-through raincoats and unusual shoes and the usual mixture of locals in coloured anoraks and trainers. Some of the girls, mostly students, Jakub noticed, were lovely, and he'd watch them as they'd stop and scrutinise each picture. He knew they were judging what would be an appropriate time to devote to each the way they'd stop and stare, scanning every inch of the canvas, though sometimes they'd just keep walking. Many of them stopped at 'The Vision After the Sermon' and they often turned to each other and smiled. Perhaps they too thought angels wrestling was a rather strange idea, but he'd never know, for after an initial acknowledgement that he was there, they rarely looked at him again. Nancy McDonald was next door and he knew she'd be bursting for a fag about then but fags were the last thing on his mind. He smiled or nodded if someone looked at him but in repose, his eyes seemed constantly to settle on the Jacob picture. Sometimes stretching his legs, he'd half close his eyes as you do in sunlight and he'd see the women's headgear as blobs of white against the dancing red. He even found himself once trying to look elsewhere as if he'd been staring at a woman and she'd noticed and turned.

Folk rarely spoke to Jakub but one afternoon a young girl with long red hair walked towards him and asked if it was true that Gauguin himself was in the angel picture. Jakub shifted uneasily, rose and walked with her slowly towards the picture. He had no idea what Gauguin looked like or if any one of the figures was Gauguin, but he felt he had some kind of duty to satisfy her. He turned to her and pointed at the dark figure with the beard being throttled by the angel.

'That is him,' he said, with as much conviction as he could muster, 'That man there.'

She smiled and said she didn't think Gauguin had a beard, but Jakub opened his hands and said 'That is art. Not easy to understand.' Jakub smiled. She thanked him and moved on. Jakub felt good, it was the first time he'd been asked a question.

The next day he was summoned to the director's office where the bald man who'd interviewed him for the job gave him a couple of print-offs one of which had Gauguin's painting on it with a short commentary beneath.

Jakub's Angel

'Jakub, I'd like you to read through these carefully. If there are any language problems, let me know, but we pride ourselves on being able to help the public here if possible. If you're not sure about anything, send them to the information desk downstairs. If you can learn a little about the pictures, then that's well and good, but your main job here is security.' He sat back and folded his arms. 'Oh, by the way, Jakub, Gauguin's the one on the right, not the wrestler. The wrestler's Jacob. That's why it's called Jacob and the Angel.' Jakub apologised but couldn't help feeling that he was being patronised by this man. How could he be expected to know all this? And how did this man know about the girl's question? It was a puzzle.

He trudged back upstairs and saw that Nancy was straddling his rooms and her own while he was away. 'Everything OK, Jakub?' He smiled and said he'd made a mistake, but it was not bad, and resumed his stance. He couldn't understand how they'd known about the girl's question and the thought plagued him all morning. Then that afternoon the girl appeared again. This time, she walked over to him and said she was really sorry if she'd got him into any trouble. He looked at her blankly.

'It's just like, well, it's a bit embarrassing really, but my dad's (almost a whisper) like, the Director here. I just happened to mention the Gauguin picture and... well, you know the rest. I'm really, really, sorry.' Jakub was astonished but collected himself and got up. He offered his hand.

'I apologise to you please. I made the mistake, I am thinking.' He felt a smile cross his face. She smiled also.

'I don't come very often', she said, 'Get a bit sick of Art- talk at home to be honest, but Dad's coughed up for my rent so I thought I'd make the effort, and here I am. I'm Verity by the way.'

Jakub looked at her. She looked at him, tilted her head. 'So what's your name?'

'Oh. Jakub.'
'Very funny.'
'It is funny? Why?'
'Oh God. Talk about digging holes. No, I mean the picture. The Jacob in the picture… and you - both kind of Jacob.'
'Ah. Yes. Funny.'
She hovered a moment, said 'Bye then,' and walked off.

That night Jakub couldn't sleep. In his dreams, a red-haired girl in a headsquare came into the post office and bought some stamps. Then he was walking with her through Blonia Common where they threw bread to the ducks. She never stopped looking at him. He could feel her thin fingers in his….

He woke, exhausted. He'd overslept, but by a miracle caught his usual bus and arrived on time for work. All that day his eyes darted to one or the other doors of his gallery at the sound of steps. She didn't come and his legs ached.

For several weeks, Jakub felt a turmoil he'd never experienced before but gradually the memory of her face faded and he began to regain his life. The notes he'd been given he'd tried but failed to concentrate on, but now at last he managed. He learned and relearned about the key paintings in the rooms and by day studied every picture when things were quiet. For a time, they moved him to Galleries One, Two and Three downstairs, but he soon found himself back in his favourite spot.

Just as the Gallery was about to close one day she came back. She was wearing jeans and a green flowery dress with big brown boots. His heart leapt, but he stayed quite still and tried to avoid looking at her. There was another couple in the room and they were staring at the Jacob picture. Out of the corner of his eye, he saw her bend and whisper something to them. He looked away and stared at a landscape by Pissarro.

He heard a laugh from the couple and they wandered away. She was sitting on the sofa in the middle of the room staring at the Gauguin.

'Jakub,' she wasn't looking at him. 'I think you look like the man with the angel. Cut off his beard and it could be you.'

He turned, his heart pounding. Just the sound of her voice had taken him back to the heart of the flames. He didn't know what to say.

'Why are they wrestling anyway?' she said. 'Oh don't tell me, he's made some stupid crack about people with wings I suppose.' She laughed. He ambled over to her, calm now, controlled, but inside he was eager to show her his newly-acquired knowledge.

'Jacob is wrestling with God. Not really God, but in his head, you see.' He didn't look at her but added, 'Jacob hurt his hip.'

'You're making it up again, aren't you? His hip? Come on!' She laughed.

'No. No. Now I know this.'

'OK. So it's a metaphor for some sort of spiritual struggle then. I get it. Don't get the hip bit though. How can you damage your hip struggling with your conscience?'

Jakub shrugged. 'Who knows. It is art.' He smiled again. She was looking at him in the way he remembered and he felt again as if something was rising in his chest, chill sweat dribbling from his armpits. He walked back to his seat by the door and she followed him and perched on the floor beside him. Under his shirt, his heart was going crazy. He was finding it hard to breathe. He could see how scuffed her leather boots were. Krakow girls' boots. For an age neither spoke. He wondered what they would think – him sitting here with this girl at his feet.

'Do you like working here?'

'Yes. It's a good job.' He smiled. This was better, just talk.

'Are you married?'

'Me? No. Who would marry me?'

'Someone. Someday maybe. Can't see myself getting married, come to that. Why tie yourself down.'

'Love.'

'Oh, that old thing.'

'You don't believe in love, Verity?'

'I believe in having fun.'

Jakub didn't know what to say. A bell went. He stood up.

'Oh God, I'm late again! Always bloody late. See you, Jakub.'

She ran off. He watched her disappear down the carpeted stairs. Nancy appeared and shook her head.

'That kid thinks she owns this place,' she said, offering Jakub a toffee caramel from her pocket. 'Don't let them see you chewing.'

A week later she came again. This time, she didn't look at any of the pictures but settled down beside him and opened her bag. She took out a baguette and offered it to him.

'I can't eat here,' he said, 'You must know this.'

'Well, if you don't have it the gulls will. Take it for later.' She disappeared waving a floppy arm. It was tuna which he hated. He put it below his seat and when his shift was over he placed it in the locker room bin.

He hadn't been sleeping again. Every waking moment he saw her in her dress and her big boots. She reminded him of some of the Polish girls he'd seen at the University across from the post office, long-haired, confident, always laughing and always with those good-looking boys, smoking their cheroots and talking, always talking over their beer.

Hope settled on Jakub like a fly on a cake. It shouldn't be there. It only tarnished, soiled, but couldn't be swatted. It flew off, but returned,, each time with more purpose it seemed. He told Mal eventually, and he laughed. 'Go for it, man, she likes you,' but Jakub didn't believe him. Mal's girlfriend Rhona was less encouraging. She told Jakub not to get carried away. 'She's just one of those girls who like to flirt. It makes them feel good to get some attention. She knows you fancy her. I don't mean to be rude, but she's rich, Jakub, why would she bother with an ordinary Gallery assistant? Next time she comes tell her you're busy. She's only playing with you.' Mal gave her a look and ordered another round.

Not long after, Jakub was moved to the print room. Dimly lit and subterranean, he felt he had sunk to the bottom of the sea. Occasionally he'd censure a visitor for touching the glass while pointing out some feature of a print but apart from that there were no questions down here and he missed the colours. He wondered if he could keep going, for just entering the building each day was the fly settling.

Then she came again. She wafted through with a boy in tow, pointed to a couple of prints and was gone. She hadn't even acknowledged his presence. He felt an itch in his right instep, took off his shoe and scratched. When he looked up, she was there in front of him. He could smell her scent. He was flustered, and with some difficulty, replaced his shoe.

'Hello. It's me again. Bad pennies and all that.'

'You are a fly on a cake.' He turned his head away from her.

'What?'

'Old Polish proverb. Don't swat a fly on a cake.'

'Give me time and I'll come up with a Scottish one. My God. I'm a fly. I'd no idea Poles were so profound. You could flick it off I suppose without doing too much damage to the icing or whatever.'

'Perhaps,' said Jakub, 'but it would be a risk. Now I have to go soon.' He looked up at her face. 'Mr McKenzie will be taking over. Come with me, please. I need to talk to you.' He ushered her into a dim corner and with a lungful of courage, found the words he needed.

'Verity you are a very pretty girl. Why do you talk to me? Why do you want to hurt me?' He couldn't look at her.

'Hurt you? Jakub I don't want to hurt you. Jesus, where does this come from? I like you. Is that a crime? My father seems to think it is, by the way.'

'Your father?'

'Yes, my father. I told him about you. He made me promise I wouldn't talk to you again or you'd have to go.' She stood closer to him and took his hand. 'I can't eat, Jakub. I can't study, I can't read, I can't do a bloody thing for thinking about you. What can I do?' She took his hand.

'Two flies.'

'Oh shut up about the bloody flies will you. It's me I'm talking about. Me and you.' She let his hand fall and bent her head. Her fingers were over her eyes. When she removed them, the tips were wet.

'Do you like ducks?' he said. 'Perhaps, Verity, we will feed some ducks together.'

AUTHENTICITY

Prentice's knee bumped the desk and he looked at his watch again. Time playing its games, its quick-slow games. He didn't care if they noticed. What did it matter? They knew he didn't want to be here either. For him, it was a duty, punishment for them. There were three of them today, all well-kent faces: McLeod, Hickey and…he checked the girl…Eva Fraser. He'd put McLeod near the front and left the other two to sit further back. No audience for our friend. They'd all started writing.

There was a large black and white poster of Paris on the back wall and he remembered the argument with Sarah in the restaurant. She'd been flirting with their waiter, complimenting him on his English, even touched his wrist at one stage. It wouldn't have mattered if he hadn't been good-looking but when the bastard gave her that rose he'd flipped into a mood which lasted long after the meal. She said every woman got a rose stupid, and maybe they did, but he felt she'd betrayed him as if he wasn't enough for her. They strode along the Left Bank past the shuttered wooden stalls and he'd never felt so lonely. Oh, it was okay soon after but she still couldn't resist turning on the charm when an attractive man was near and it irked him still.

He opened the desk drawer and saw a bottle of nail varnish, a mirror, tissues, a box full of felt tips, all neatly arranged. It reminded him of the organs in a rat's body that he'd once seen exposed: everything in its own neat little space. All those weird colours each different in texture but all belonging together: a perfect machine. Definitely a woman's drawer. There was a faint hint of scent from the seat which he liked but he couldn't put a face to whose seat it might be. It was a large staff, but it was probably one of those fat dears that sat near the far window and yakked endlessly. It was odd sitting at another teacher's desk: the seat of power, the throne from which proclamations were issued and progress determined. He thought of a picture he'd once seen of American soldiers in Saddam's throne room lounging about with their boots on the furniture taken out of their little lives in their despoliation of big ones. Not that he was despoiling anything, but here he was sitting in this prim woman's seat and something inside made him want to put his feet up on the desk. The desk was so tidy. He imagined what sitting in the Head's chair would be like, his feet up on the desk and pushing his buzzer to admit some sad little soul for punishment. Not that there was much of that these days he mused. Punishment? This was as bad as it got. Sitting in a warm classroom writing an essay with your pals. All in it together. Okay, the others have gone home, but it won't be long before they're home too.

He had only been here a couple of terms but his own desk was a mess of papers and jotters. He never seemed able to find space to put things and every day more pieces of paper appeared. Never lift a piece of paper twice, they said which made sense, but he just couldn't do it. Every day he'd pick up something, glance at it, decide it wasn't important but on the other hand, he'd probably need it later, so down it went in the same place. His top drawer was filled with rubbers, pencils, post-its of various shades, a couple of confiscated pen-knives, paperclips, rubber bands and a dirty mag he'd taken from a second year after much protest about civil rights. Now and then he peeked at it then paid a visit to the staff toilet. He kept reminding himself to get rid of it but never had. Fraser, his Principal Teacher, had said he'd order him a set of filing trays because they'd be useful. Point taken.

Authenticity

The late sun which had brightened his left hand had moved to the book now. Time was working after all. He opened a copy of "L'Etranger" which was lying on the desk - a book he'd read years before. He flicked through it, closed it and put it down. Their heads were all down and they scribbled away silently. The sun caught "Camus" and he stared at the word till he became mesmerised by it, then lost it, then saw it again, not as the message but as the sign. He wrote his own name on a scrap of paper and looked at it. "Alastair Prentice." That was him. All he was. Not the name: there would be many with that name, but the way he wrote it made it him and no other. That has always been him, that movement of the fingers and arm that was unique. For a second or two he was lost in the shape and the sound of himself, wondering what it would feel like to be another shape, another sound. Not to be him at all. Not to be the butt of jokes about Mr A. Prentice the new English teacher who was just learning his trade. Ha ha! He remembered his father teaching him to write his signature. "No Son, you've got to make it unique - don't just write it neatly, make it flow, give it some style." He practised and in the end it was just like his father's. A hand was up.

'Yes?'
'Paper.'
'Yes?'
'Paper.'
'Paper what?'
'Aeroplanes.' The boy laughed, turning round for confirmation that his joke was appreciated. He was a hulking creature with hands that made the pencil look tiny. Prentice had the feeling he'd entered a linguistic cul-de-sac. Bugger this, he thought and went into reverse.

'Please?' Prentice prayed.

'Oh aye, pleeeese..' came from the boy whose cheeks expanded in exaggerated fashion as he squeezed out the word. 'Please Mr Prentice can I have more paper. Please.'

If he said it often enough, it would mask any climb down. He was a pro.

'Come and get it.'

The boy eased himself up from his tiny desk making as much din as possible. He reached Prentice's desk and snatched the paper, an old attendance bulletin.

'And John, when you sit down, don't move the desk.' The minute he said it he realised his mistake. New man, new errors. Would he ever learn? He kept his head down. Sure enough, the desk rasped. He said nothing. He could imagine the grin. Some threats were roads that ended in cliffs. Punishment seemed to gulp down punishment till the only ones punished were those who cared.

He heard a distant car alarm from across the street and wished he himself there, out in the sun, waiting for his bus home. It was Sarah's week for the car. Detention. Once a month he had to be here watching over the club, sensing in the hanging silence a companionship he'd never known. The system detained him: duty, doing the right thing, treading the marriage path carefully.

Eva could go early the note said, and Thomas should go after forty minutes. Minor misdemeanours. The word came to him, a word from another age; a word whose meaning was unworthy of its grandeur. Too long to signify the sudden expletives, the violence, the quick anger that cared nothing for what might follow. God knows what McLeod had done.

From far away he caught the faint tinny rattle and looked up. The headphones were plugged into McLeod's ear and his right paw jerked to the beat.

'Off. Put it away.' The voice roused itself reluctantly... 'NOW!' It was a game of bait the hook, catch the authority fish. And the fish knew it. Notice me. Notice me being bad because that's what I'm good at. It was a trap every teacher knew, but few could avoid when it was set. The watch again. Twenty minutes left.

'Eve, Thomas, you can go.'

Authenticity

A great clatter of bags, a slap of commiseration for John from Hickey on his way out. Prentice opened the book and tried to read.

'How do you spell futret?'

'Futret?' The sound baffled him for a moment then he remembered a TV programme he'd seen the week before.

'I think you mean ferret. F-E-R-R-E-T' Letter by letter the boy wrote it down.

'Ta.'

The word hit the air like a droplet of water in an ice storm. The fat crack of the "a" hung for an age in Prentice's brain. Was he hearing things? He looked up. His tongue couldn't be halted…

'Are you writing about ferrets?'

'Aye.'

'You've got one, have you? At home?'

'Three.'

He knew the boy lived in the sticks and that his father was a gamekeeper or something. He knew those connections that spark contact, the shared experience. He knew but he didn't care. Fuck it, why should he bother with this idiot who'd never given anything but trouble in classes. He stared at the boy, who stopped writing and looked up. There was a flush on the boy's cheeks when he spoke.

'Ah'm needin rid of one.'

'Oh, why is that?'

'Two's enough for the burrows that are left. They're building on the land. I'll let you have one if you want.'

Prentice looked down at the book in front of him, taken aback by the turn the conversation had taken. A ferret. What the hell would he do with a ferret? He had a flashing image of an elongated furry thing which by all accounts stank to heaven. He saw Sarah's face. Something inside did a somersault.

'Free to a good home. With a box.' The boy had turned into a salesman.

'A box too. Sounds irresistible. What would I do with it?'

'Rabbits'

'Not the biggest problem I have.'

'Plenty up Braehead way. You get good money for them.'

'OK. Thanks for the offer, but I don't think I've got room for a ferret where I live.'

'Where's that?'

Cheeky bugger. What the hell…"Out Blackford way." Prentice suddenly realised he was in the middle of a dialogue but not sure how he got there. There was a tone now in the boy's voice that had crossed over that barrier that disrespect builds. His voice was gentler, more polite as if some switch had been flicked. Prentice was touched that this boy could be different; not aggressive, surly, impertinent, provocative - the convenient labels that put him in his box, but human. That was it simply: he could be human.

'Is it time yet?' the boy enquired? Prentice checked his watch. Five minutes left. He'd let him go early. Some little gesture for a change in attitude.

'Okay, we'll call it a day there. Bring out your essay.'

The essay was in front of him face down before he realised that this time the desk had made no noise. He turned over the paper and read:

'I don't like school. I'm sitting here writing words cos smigsy asked for it better of being at hame with the dogs and the ferrets. I'll feed them sops then take them up the brae Charlie needs more bunnies he says.'

He had written the same paragraph over and over.

'Couldnae think of anything else tae write.'

'Well, at least you've got something you really like, eh? If you hate school, at least you love your dogs and your futtrets.'

'Oh, I've thought of something else. Can I write it now?'

'Of course.'

Prentice was conscious of a strong animal odour from the boy who bent over him and wrote *'and I asked Mr Prentis if he wanted one of my ferrets but he didn't.'*

'That's finished.'

'You make me sound a bit cruel… John isn't it? It's not that I don't like ferrets…'

'Well then. She'll be going to a good home.'

Prentice pulled the papers together, tapped them on the desk twice and looked up to see a grin he hadn't seen before. A hardness had gone from the stare. Neither spoke. John turned and strode to the door.

'Oh John, you've forgotten to write your name on this. Mr Wilson needs that.'

He returned and wrote his name very carefully. ***John McLeod.'***

'That's me,' he said proudly and left the room.

DAFFODILS

Russell Birch spotted them the moment he stepped off the train. Daffodils. Bunches of daffodils bright as butter, on a stall by the exit. He saw a young man walk away with a bunch but Russell, brought up to feel uneasy exposing the affection such a gift symbolises, knew he could never carry a bunch home for Ailsa. Through the train window earlier, the blur of April fields fled over his shoulder, blotches of faint yellow spreading a flickering light as the daffodils emerged, slow as ever, here in the North. In the train he'd observed the carmine nails of the woman opposite him as she held up her newspaper, caught the movement below him where the blue chisel-tip of her shoe bobbed under the table. He remembered how sexy a woman's discarded shoes had seemed to him in that hotel room years before, the beige soles a skin that hinted moisture, the act of stepping free of them the prologue to their little play. He felt a frisson of remembered lust that disappeared as the paper cut on his finger touched his briefcase.

Now he's here again in the clamour of the station. The smell of coffee, the click of the Arrivals and Departures boards, the hiss of released brakes, the upturned eyes, the breathless anxiety that makes the air heavy and exciting; the sweet scent as he passes, of daffodils proffered hesitantly by the red-faced man. 'Daffies, fresh daffies. For the little lady in your life.'

It was Wednesday now and the previous Thursday, there had been a sense of things coming to a head. They'd all been on edge for weeks in the office: who'd go, who'd stay, was all the talk. "Compression." That was the word Inman used. There's always a new word for it - language dodging and weaving. Get rid of some middle-management and you're back on an even keel. No room for passengers. Bastards.

He was the second oldest next to Bill, the others young, two of them bald and trendy, shiny bright with ambition. They'd stay, every word and gesture carefully crafted to please, while he'd forgotten how. The body had developed rattles and shudders like an old car, and old ideas had become as redundant as old skin. His wife always seemed to want him to change: Why don't you, this, why don't you, that, was the litany to which there was no reply that she ever heard, but in his head he fought back loud and clear like the bullied child who gives the bully a thrashing every night in his dreams. That was the trouble between them - they'd gone through dialogue and entered the land of female monologue where conversation becomes instruction. As their relationship ossified, the office sometimes seemed more attractive than home, even allowing for the political shenanigans that made him curb his tongue. At least his secretary listened to him and sometimes even laughed at his faux-rebellious antics. It wasn't enough. He felt things closing in on him: the looks, the casual remarks, the jokes against him that weren't jokes now. Well, he'd tripped and sprained his ankle, been off work for a week and it changed his rhythm, gave him a peace he hadn't had in years. Under a bush in the garden - her domain - he'd spotted a clump of light blue and purple anemones. He bent to examine them, the first time he'd really looked at a flower for years and something of their simple beauty touched him: no P.R. required, just their own perfection. He realised how far he'd fallen, into a world where notions of beauty related to the size of contracts or the sway of a secretary's behind.

He was called back at half-past two that afternoon. There were two of them there - Inman and Smith, the accountant. Smith opened the door and told him to take a seat while Inman shook his head like a headmaster faced with a recalcitrant pupil.

'Russell, there are times when I hate this business.' It didn't take him long to get to the point. He was terribly sorry, and all that crap but times were hard and difficult decisions had to be made.

'It's about making room, Russell - new ideas, new ways of thinking. Oh, you will make sure you leave your BlackBerry.' He knew the drill: the box, the minder, in case he ran amok, buggering up the computer system or something, though he doubted they'd think him capable of that. To them, the suddenness made amputation painless: a bloodless slaughter. He closed the door behind him and felt as if he'd been held underwater then let up to the surface, gagging for air, every cell in him shuddering from the onslaught. Guantanamo stuff. He'd said nothing. They seemed disappointed.

As he moved, it was as if everything he saw was about to flip from present to past: the blue carpet under his feet; the creak half-way along the corridor; the hairline crack in the glass on Jackson's window; the drinks dispenser with its coffee breath. Smith had mouthed the usual platitudes as they walked to his room, how they'd sort out the financial side to his advantage, no worries on that score. The usual. Then quite quickly he regained his calm. I'm okay. A bit shocked, but okay. Better than I thought. Perhaps it'll hit me later…perhaps this is it, and I won't feel any worse. He saw himself on a CCTV in his head, walking purposefully, opening the door to his office, moving towards his desk – "That's him! That's the guy we shed!"

Smith stood outside the door, said he'd give him a few minutes, the hell with protocol. Russell stroked the glass on his wife's photo, then kissed it. She disappeared, reappeared, her smile intact. He didn't know why he'd done it. He'd hoped that's what would happen when he told her, that she'd end up smiling, feeling some sympathy for him but he doubted it. He thought of the new kitchen she wanted, could see her beaming over the brochure. She seemed so far away. He wondered where she would be at

Daffodils

this moment. Now everything he knew, everything safe had started to crack and crumble. His hands were shaking. Not really calm at all. Across the street, the dentist had been working on a patient. A man leaned forward to spit. Russell smiled. Life would go on. Had people in the building opposite often seen him at the window? Had he become a kind of norm for them? Would they miss him when he went? He wanted to be missed, for them to turn and say 'I haven't seen that man at the window for a few days.' Cast a shadow, however small. As a child would erase an unsatisfactory drawing - head, arms, body, legs, then nothing, he felt himself obliterated. There were office sounds now. Word would surely be out. He wondered where his secretary was. She knew about the down-sizing and they'd talked about it over coffee one morning. He was too hard an act to follow she said, but he knew differently.

The lift slowed, juddered to a halt, and he stepped into the foyer. It was raining, a thin drizzle that had sprouted umbrellas. He nodded to Archie on the front desk before making his way out into the street, hoped no-one would realise the significance of the box. Got to get rid of it, he thought, so he went into the first pub he saw, sloped into the stinking toilet and stuffed everything he could into his briefcase. He flushed some papers down the pan then trampled the box flat. He took out his pen and wrote "George Inman of Wood Communications is a paedophile. Phone 688455 ext 34" on the door, above a very serviceable drawing of a vagina. That felt good.

In the brown gloom of a bar, he downed two pints of Guinness. More than once his eyes moved to the stopped clock behind the bar as if he had to be somewhere. He watched the two barmen tilt their heads for orders, eyeing the glasses as they pulled the handles. It struck him how mechanical their actions were - going through the same movements day by day, knowing exactly where everything was: the gin, the whiskies, the tequila; knowing the touch of glasses, the weight of bottles. It was a choreography to a music of gush and clink. He imagined the mechanics of his own life: the domestic rituals, then the drive to the station, park, wait for train, get on train, sit by window if possible, look through papers, attempt the Sudoku, get off train, flash his pass, walk down steps, down street, up in lift. Every day his actions were the same and now they had ceased. He wished he had stopped them, not Inman. Anyway, he mused, it's past.

Now, days later, he's still in the city, here in a deep-fried cafe, hearing the minutes move, the day sighing away. He's become a time-watcher. Ailsa expected him to be somewhere and he is. She expected him to get the eight-o-five and that's what he does but he can't keep this up for long. Every day the sand is running out on this lie. Each night he goes home determined to tell her but he doesn't. This would be another brick in the monument she was constructing to his inadequacy: can't be faithful, useless at man-things, and now can't keep a job. She's begun to disappear as the person who once loved him. So here he is again, still in the city, killing time. He's thought of getting off the train at one of the stations on the way but he doesn't know how he would spend the day. At least here he can sit in a cafe or go to a museum or art gallery. Killing it, passing it, time is on his hands like some unsightly stain.

 He sits at a cold little table with a giant laminated menu which shows a picture of a breakfast. "Full Scottish Breakfast – four-ninety-nine." Every damn thing that can go in a frying pan. How could you walk after eating that! Eight-forty-five in the morning. He should be scanning his mail, sipping scalding coffee from his Partick Thistle mug. No-one here but him. Well, who would be here? The woman has acknowledged him with a smile as if any small word would make him a regular. Habit again, he thinks. There are a thousand cafes in this city and I have to come here every day. He opens his case and takes out the beginnings of the C.V. he started two days ago, looks at what he's written and a surging anger overcomes him. He puts it back in his case, but closes it too quickly and one of the pages spills on the table. Calm down. Calm down. He won't do it. Sell himself. What's the point? Start again in some new place where he knows no-one? The chances of being paid on the same scale were zero. He's fifty-five years old, with a dodgy prostate, backache, footache, a sliced finger and a battered ego.

'Y'okay chum?'

He looks up into a ruddy face with laughing eyes. The man is built like a gorilla with a neck wider than his head.

'You alright chum?'

'Oh, I'm fine, thanks.'

'Right y'are then.'

He wonders what he must look like; takes off his tie and stuffs it in his pocket. His feet are burning. He watches the man, cutlery sticking out from his top pocket, carry his plate and cup to a table by the window, take the paper from under his arm and prop it against the sauce. Russell envies him his gross contentment. Did he have a job? He wonders what the man would say if he told him he'd lost his job. Go and get another one chum. I've a pal that might have something for you.

That James Taylor song about being lonely tonight starts playing. Why is it that every damn song he hears seems to poke the wound of his predicament? Well, this is his new routine: the cafe till for as long as he can spin out his coffee then down the street to the Museum of Modern Art where he's even started reading the notes on the pictures, into the nearest pub, then walk, then another cafe. He can't keep this up much longer.

Outside The Museum, the horseman has a traffic cone on his noble head. He always seems to have a traffic cone on his head as if they've given up trying to keep him cone-free. That stern chiselled face under a dunce's cap. He sees Inman with a cone on his head, the bubble of his pomposity burst, thinks how great it would be to pull it down and down till the cone **was** Inman's stupid head. The sun comes out, suddenly, as it does in this city and he wonders if there will be daffodils in Kelvingrove Park. There'll be space there to breathe at least, grass, views.

On the steep grassy slopes below the Victorian terrace, he finds his bright solace. He zigzags his way up the path and sits on a bench. He feels his heart pumping. There's no-one about. He unlaces his shoes and lets his feet rest on them, clear of the cigarette stubs. He can feel his feet expanding. A fly moves from his shoulder and settles on his left foot for a moment. The sandwich he bought the previous day now smells even stronger so he throws it in the bin then jumps as his phone suddenly bursts into its tinny Mozart tune. It's a text message:

'Edwin. I love U v much. Just
so U know. Ailsa.'

He watches the breeze push the daffodils, their shapes changing. He thinks of Ailsa, of change. She's recently begun driving him to the station as she needs the car "for little things." He could easily catch the bus home from the station, couldn't he? She's taken to phoning him in the afternoons asking what he'd like for tea, would he bring this or that, even asking if the rain was really heavy there. She's mellowed a little in the weeks since she'd gone to her Spanish class, but the politeness that has shaped their exchanges for years still holds and he tells himself her warmth is a temporary blip. Ailsa texting him with that. Like some schoolgirl's message, keyed under a desk, he thinks. He's moved, can't remember her ever texting him, something she's picked up from their grandchildren. He switches the phone off and holds it for some time, limp in his hands, letting the simple words wash over him: "…so U know."

In front of him, the brightness of the daffodils and the wild garlic is vivid against the grey city offices sprawling beyond. It's an April day and here he is to see this, to be told his wife loves him. She does love him and he needs to know. His chest heaves as if something like the great slow clouds above him have shifted deep inside. He hopes no-one will come by now.

He remembers Inman's words: "Make room."

'You're right, Inman, you prick. I'll make some fucking room.' He takes the papers from his case and rips them up before putting them in the bin. His stupid novel thrown away, he moves towards the grass.

All the way home on the train the sun pierces banks of cloud, tipping them pink. Horses cavort round a muddy paddock and at a station his eyes linger on a couple of teenagers on a bench, hand in hand, lost in each other. He finds himself drumming on his case. No pain. The finger's healing. He can't wait to see Ailsa now, tell her everything. Now he really can imagine her smiling at him as she did in that photo. He can do it. He will.

At the usual time, his train pulls into the neat little station with its hanging baskets hinting of colour again. He mounts the steps over the line and is surprised to see Ailsa standing beside the car. With a flourish, she opens the door for him.

'What are you doing here?'

'A surprise. Chauffeur driven. Or is it chauffeuse? Why don't we go for a drink for a change.' He gets in the car. She smells garlic.

'Good idea,' he says, touching her knee. She turns, smiling.

'What's that smell? '

'Ha.'

'You've bought me flowers.'

'In a way.'

He opens his case and a buttery light bathes her face.

Printed in Great Britain
by Amazon